# CRAFT

# CRAFT

ANANDA LIMA

# STORIES I WROTE FOR THE DEVIL

**TOR**

TOR PUBLISHING GROUP

NEW YORK

This is a work of fiction. All of the characters, organizations, and events portrayed in this novel are either products of the author's imagination or are used fictitiously.

CRAFT: STORIES I WROTE FOR THE DEVIL

A Tor Book
Published by Tom Doherty Associates / Tor Publishing Group
120 Broadway
New York, NY 10271

www.torpublishinggroup.com

Tor® is a registered trademark of Macmillan Publishing Group, LLC.

The Library of Congress Cataloging-in-Publication Data is available upon request.

ISBN 978-1-250-29297-1 (hardcover)
ISBN 978-1-250-29299-5 (ebook)

Our books may be purchased in bulk for promotional, educational, or business use. Please contact your local bookseller or the Macmillan Corporate and Premium Sales Department at 1-800-221-7945, extension 5442, or by email at MacmillanSpecialMarkets@macmillan.com.

First Edition: 2024

Printed in the United States of America

0   9   8   7   6   5   4   3   2   1

FOR NOAH, DAN AND ALI

FOR THE DEVIL

*There's a war going on. The battlefield's in the mind.*
*And the prize is the soul.*

PRINCE, 1999 YAHOO! INTERNET LIFE
ONLINE MUSIC AWARDS


*Everyone on television was screaming all the time.*

MASHA GESSEN,
*THE FUTURE IS HISTORY*

# STORIES I WROTE FOR THE DEVIL

{ }

You probably couldn't tell by looking at her now, but once, back in her twenties, the writer had slept with the Devil. They met at a Halloween party in a pop-up art space in 1999. She wore a red dress and pillbox hat, like Nancy Reagan. Though the way the dress clung to her curves mocked the First Lady's performance of propriety. No one got it; the closest she got was "naughty Jackie O.?" But the Devil would get it. She had stood in the red and blue neon lights, holding a drink in one hand, running her finger over her fake pearls with the other, when she'd seen him across the room.

Thinking of that night now, at her desk in the bright morning light, the writer lifted her hand off the keyboard and traced her collarbone again, now bare between the top buttons of her plain denim shirt.

The writer had not been a writer then, at least not openly so. But the Devil had known. He had known the space she had inside her to carry her stories. He had known her hunger. She typed, and her young self took a sip of her drink and looked straight back into the Devil's eyes.

# RAPTURE

You probably can't tell by looking at me now, but once, back in my twenties, I slept with the Devil. We met at a Halloween party in a closed-down store space in Manhattan, Union Square, in 1981. I was nursing my third Snake Bite in the corner. Silhouettes danced to "Memorabilia," backlit by a makeshift red-and-blue-neon installation stuck to a crumbling brick wall. The Devil was sitting alone on a beat-up brown corduroy sofa. I was inauguration Nancy Reagan: a tighter version of the red Adolfo dress, black gloves, a wig between chestnut brown and dirty blond, topped with a red pillbox hat. He wore an ill-fitting suit, a faded orange wig, and some bad foundation. I walked up to him and asked what he was, yelling over the music. He said he was the future. I told him his costume sucked. He smiled and said he was often misunderstood, scanning the room as if hoping for a specific somebody else to show up. I began spinning the first thread of his story: a woman in a white dress, a cheap Halloween bride costume, would walk in holding a veil in her hand. I imagined him watching as the woman looked for someone too, but not him. As I thought this, the Devil nodded, almost imperceptibly, as if privately approving of something, but continued looking at the room with that slight sadness, that want. I recognized some of what I'd been carrying inside, mirrored on his face.

I thought my friends had stood me up. In my mind, I superimposed said friends, Michael and Angela, over the scene. Michael and Angela as I introduced them to each other at the company Christmas party the year before. Michael and Angela discreetly brushing their hands as they passed each other en route to the elevator, when I first realized they might be together. Michael and Angela the day I found them in the bathroom during lunch break. Those days, I saw Michael and Angela everywhere. I feared the two dancers in the corner, her arms over his shoulders, his pulling her by the waist, were Michael and Angela. Though it was useless to fear it now that everything was out in the open. If it weren't happening here, it would be happening somewhere else. In her bedroom, in his, in the entry hall of their apartment building because they couldn't wait, in a taxi on their way here.

I downed the rest of my drink.

"Are you waiting for someone?" I asked the Devil.

The Devil suspended his search and looked at me straight on for the first time. Something awakened in my body. Despite his ridiculous clothes, he looked like a 1940s movie star, with that strong jaw, his nose just the right amount of imperfect. It had been so long since I'd felt anything like that. Even with Michael, the hurt had coiled up around that feeling and all but strangled it. Yet here it was again, that fledgling want serpentining up my bones. I didn't want to lose it. I wanted it to stay inside me.

The Devil gave me a sly smile and complimented me on my nice family values. I held my fake pearls, feigning shyness, and sat next to him, then stretched my legs over his lap. I grabbed a cigarette and dangled it from my matte-red lips as I fumbled for my matches. He offered me a light. It was as if he held an invisible lighter: there was his hand, and there was the flame. But it was dark, and I wasn't exactly sober. I leaned in. He moved the fire an inch away from my reach and said I could just say no, smiling as if it were some kind of inside joke. I didn't know what he was on about, but I had always liked dorks. I pulled his hand toward my cigarette and inhaled.

A heat fluttered up from my fingertips where they touched him. It was so unexpectedly pleasant, the sparkling sensation on my skin, the warmth rising through my veins up to my palms. I let go of his hands while I still could. I took off my red pillbox hat, my Nancy wig, fluffed up my hair. I'd recently cut it like Kim Wilde, though my hair was brown. I slid his wig off, revealing his immaculate black hair slicked back. I covered it with Nancy's hair while facing him, our mouths inches away as I adjusted the wig and topped it with the red hat. Remaining close, I stared into him and put his orange wig on myself. He didn't look away as other men would have. Blondie's "Rapture" started playing. Our lips were on the verge of touching. Deep in his eyes (had they been green?), the reflection of the red neon looked like fire.

I might have stayed there, trapped in the darkness, in the fire. But someone tapped me on the shoulder, and I came back to my body. They had come after all. Angela was dressed up as Princess Diana, Michael as Prince Charles, their hands glued together as usual. Angela adjusted her tiara, leaning into Michael. Their costumes were brilliant, and my heartbeat was choking me. I wanted to vomit.

"And you are?" Angela asked the Devil.

The Devil answered he was the Devil.

"What happened to the future?" I asked.

He said the future was his costume, but who he was was the Devil.

"What's the difference?" Angela asked.

"And you." Michael looked at me, my red dress and the orange wig. "Fire?"

"A dumpster fire," I replied.

Michael and Angela laughed, a little uncomfortably.

The Devil nodded as he repeated the phrase "dumpster fire," then said he would have to steal it.

"You look great." Angela smiled at me, but her eyes were filled with pity. Maybe to spare me from seeing it, she looked away. She put her free hand on my shoulder for a few seconds, then moved it away.

The Devil said he'd always liked red as his hand ran up my calf to the back of my knee, just under the hem of my dress. He said, slowly, that red was a picker-upper. My face contorted, overwhelmed with pleasure. He broke contact, and I opened my eyes just in time to notice Angela's and Michael's confused looks moving between my leg and my face, then looking away, a little embarrassed. *Thank you,* I thought. The Devil stood up and whispered in my ear that I was welcome, then told us he would get us some drinks.

Michael had his hands in his pockets. Angela crossed her arms and rubbed her elbows gently. They looked away awkwardly for a few seconds as if they needed time to reassess how to see me. Gradually, they leaned into each other again and looked at me anew.

I wished I could hate them then. But I didn't. I loved Angela and was in love with Michael. But I resented that they hadn't been a little kinder to me over the whole thing. And that they'd left me waiting for them in a sketchy party where the Devil could proposition me, steal me away. But the Devil hadn't done either of these things. What was the deal?

"So?" Angela asked in a mock conspiratorial tone.

"So?" I played coy.

"Tell me more about Prince Charming." She let go of Michael and joined me on the sofa, locking arms with me.

Michael followed, smiling dimly.

"There's not much to tell," I said, pretending there was much to tell. Except that, supposedly, he was the Devil, I thought.

Somewhere on the opposite side of the room, someone had turned on a fog machine. The room smelled sweet and chemical.

The Devil winked at me as he walked back into the room, a pyramid with four old-fashioneds on his right hand, on his left hand, a flaming B-52.

He leaned down to the sofa where the three of us were sitting now and offered me the burning drink, a long straw turned toward my lips, the flames somehow blowing in the opposite direction. He handed Michael and Angela their glasses, placed the other two on the table, and sat on the armchair beside me. After the first sip, I thought I might throw up. But the Devil reached in and lightly touched my stomach. It felt like flowers were blossoming inside me, emanating from where he had touched. The nausea was gone.

Unprompted, he told me it really was him. He was what he was.

In the space across the room, people danced to the end of "Primary" by the Cure: a couple; a group of five in a circle, jumping up and down; and several lone figures moving slowly but somehow in rhythm. The fog was thick and made them look like shadows walking in front of an old movie projector or the shapes on the walls when the power went out and my aunt used a flashlight to tell us stories. As they danced, I imagined the beginning of their story. Each of them would have lost something: the person in the middle had a recent breakup, the next one a job, the one in the corner a friend, whom she had visited in the hospital for months. Maybe they were all here, unknowingly, to meet the Devil. The Devil himself, the real one, as he had just told me, who was watching me now, pleased.

"Why do you keep saying that?" I shouted over the music.

He said he liked being honest.

"That's not what I hear."

He shook his head and looked away from me, as if a little disappointed. After a few seconds, he sighed, looked back at me, and began talking again. He said I should reconsider my sources. History was written by the victors, scapegoating, etc. "Boys Don't Cry" came on, to squeals of approval on the dance floor. The Devil had perfect teeth. As he talked, he had this look, a wounded look under the slight frown. His eyebrows were perfect. I wanted to run my fingers over them. I leaned just a little closer, wondering what he would smell like. And he was so tall, I thought. Like Michael.

The song ended and this time was not followed by another straightaway. It felt quiet for a second. Then, as if someone had turned up the volume of the ambient noise in the room: A woman dragged a chair to sit with a new group forming next to us. Loud laughter broke out from a loose circle of people waiting on the dance floor. "No! No! Not true!" said a tall skinny guy, also laughing. The fog had mostly dissipated.

The Devil wanted to know what was so special about Michael.

Michael had spilled a little of his drink on Angela's leg and tried to wipe it off with his sleeves. They both laughed. With his hair like that, he did look a little bit like Prince Charles, though skirting the opposite side of the ugliness threshold, like a good-looking actor begrudgingly made to play Prince Charles. Angela messed up his hair, and it pained me. Why her? Why was I not enough? They locked arms and drank in a pretend nuptial toast. I countered the Devil by asking what the Devil would be doing there, hanging out with me.

A song finally came on: "Faith" (someone was on a Cure bender). But the tempo was much slower than the previous songs, and the people dispersed from the informal dance area into the rest of the party, except for three stragglers, eyes closed, as they slowly danced to the long intro.

The Devil continued: It was his favorite night, he got around, it'd been a good year, he too deserved to celebrate, yadda, yadda, yadda. He didn't seem to want to get into his devilish ways. He paused. I stepped closer, feeling an urge to nuzzle into his neck like a feral but needy kitten. Plus, he said, he liked spending time with kindred spirits.

"Meaning?" I frowned. I might have been a little messed up at that moment, but I wasn't Devil level. I was not evil.

He sighed, paused, looked at me, and said he was not evil. Then he continued moving through each point as quickly as he had been before: He was often, lazily, offered up as a solution to the problem of evil. But he wasn't it at all.

I squinted at him and said I was more interested in what he had meant by "kindred spirits."

He apologized for the rant (he didn't even like talking about himself, preferred to listen, but this, pet peeve, sore spot, etc.). Then he told me what he meant: He also tended to want most what he couldn't have.

I looked at Michael, and the snake coiled tighter inside me.

The Devil put a hand on my shoulder and loosened the snake's grip just enough so I could keep breathing.

Pardon me if things get a little fuzzy from here on. All this was decades ago, and things get distorted like a cassette tape jammed and unraveled. Sometimes I feel like my memories merge a little with dreams, movies, music clips, maybe just absorbing their atmosphere, the shape of their threads, their hopes. And I'm sure I had some trouble remembering that night, even the next day. Boy, could I drink then. I was so young; in the pictures my face has that aura, that thing you can see clearly when looking at old pictures of celebrities when they were younger in those "look at how they aged" posts, some magical glow sparkling from their full cheeks. Also, in my old pictures, there's a sadness in my eyes, though I wonder if anyone other than me can detect it. I can almost feel it, a phantom pain that allows me to imagine it, even though I can't conjure it back completely.

I remember the red light in the room. One of the red bulbs in the corner started flickering halfway through the night. I remember closing my eyes for a few seconds, spreading myself from the sway of the alcohol, inhaling and exhaling as I heard the voices: the Devil, Michael, and Angela. I can still hear the Devil, his calm radio-host voice asking someone (who had he asked?) what their story was. I remember the four of us doing shots together and laughing. Angela and Michael warmed up to the Devil. He had his ways. The four of us danced to "Tainted Love." The Devil was a great dancer, goofy in the right way. Michael somehow had the Nancy wig now. Angela was still in Diana's. They were already becoming the same person. The Devil flicked his finger, and the TV turned on to MTV. It played a new song, "Thriller," though it wouldn't come out until 1982.

"The future is here," the Devil toasted.

"It's not even the future," I replied.

Angela and Michael stepped farther away, to give us some space, or maybe have each other for themselves. I put the Devil's orange wig back on him. For a second, his skin seemed to glow a strange orange, like a cheap but radioactive tan. But maybe it was the neon lights, maybe I just imagined it.

"I like him," Michael mouthed at me from across the room.

Angela nodded and gave me two thumbs up.

As I adjusted the wig, I touched the Devil's skin and felt that delicious, strange heat again. It spread, running up my arm, about to reach my elbow. I had closed my eyes. He moved away from my hand, bringing me back.

We watched Angela and Michael dance. I fantasized about asking the Devil to split them up but did not say anything.

The Devil said he could, easily, if I wanted him to.

I didn't respond, some of the heat still in my fingers.

Suddenly, Angela and Michael were arguing. I only heard fragments of what they were yelling at each other. I heard Reagan's name, and "I was just saying," and "he did nominate the first woman." I don't remember who had which position. Angela stormed out.

I walked to Michael. "What happened?"

"I don't know. She just—" He looked toward the door.

The Devil sat on the sofa, took a sip of his drink.

Then my hands were in Michael's. I was startled. There was no supernatural tingling, just his hands, but it was harder to believe than the Devil. I grabbed on, squeezed. I never wanted to leave those hands. He looked at me as he had looked at Angela earlier that night. He was moving closer. I inhaled as the snake coiled tighter in my chest. I realized I was crying. Because it was too much, and because it wasn't really happening. It wasn't Michael. It was the Devil puppeteering him.

"I love you," Michael said blindly. He didn't seem to notice I was sobbing.

I let go of him and turned to the Devil. "Stop."

The Devil shrugged.

Michael ran out after Angela.

I sat next to the Devil. He rubbed my back, careful not to touch my skin directly. I nestled my eyes on my wrists.

"It will never happen, right? I mean, for real?"

The Devil asked me what I thought. Rhetorically, he clarified.

I knew the answer.

The Devil then said I didn't have to answer him but asked if it did happen, would I still want Michael?

I began to hiccup.

The Devil told me there, there. This time, while rubbing my upper back, always over my clothes, he accidentally touched the bottom of my neck. I tingled with pleasure, suddenly wanting him.

"Would you, please?" I pointed to his finger on my neck, panting.

The Devil noticed, a little embarrassed, apologized, and moved his hand away. I rubbed my neck where he had touched it, closed my eyes, savoring the last of the warmth until it disappeared.

The Devil sat on the couch, deflated. He tried to make people happy, he really did. But it didn't work. In his eyes, the flame wilted. I could feel some of his sadness along with mine. That viscid darkness. Our two miserable, lost souls.

In the next gap between songs, I heard Angela and Michael laughing. It pained me, yet their being back together was somehow right. I gave the Devil a sorrowful smile, mirroring his. He flicked his index finger up. "Time after Time" started playing. He told me it would come out in 1983. We both took a swig of our drinks.

There was more to it, the Devil said, to the two of us being kindred spirits.

"What is it?" I asked, genuinely wanting to know the answer.

Stories, the Devil said. We both craved them.

I didn't know what the Devil meant exactly. I had not thought of myself like that before he said it. But I knew as I heard it that it was true.

"But you seem to know things. Everything."

The Devil said stories were more than knowing things, facts. There was no soul in that. It was in the telling and the words, the spaces between them.

He looked at me. I probably looked confused. He sighed and stopped talking.

I asked for elaboration, but he dismissed me with a wave of his hand, took another swig, and looked at the room. Another couple dancing very close and a group of three friends dancing out of rhythm.

We sat still, slumped side by side on the sofa until the song ended. The Devil sighed, lifted his index finger as if to pick the next song, but seemed to give up halfway through. When he lifted his finger again, it was to fill both our glasses. He looked so pathetic. I ran my hands over his wig, and it was as if I wanted to comfort us both. And in my pity for him was also growing this new compassion for me, for both of us. My pain was OK, existing as it was. I was OK. And so was everyone.

"Fuck it," I said, standing up from the couch. I calculated a clear path for us through the crowd. I would need to make it to the other side of the room, turn left for the back door, and reach far enough up the enclosed stairway where it was dark. I readied myself to make a run for it. Then I grabbed the Devil by the hand.

The heat started rising, warm little snakes uncoiling, traveling up my veins from where I touched him, wildflowers blooming from within my skin, my breath; my heart accelerated, and I walked as quickly as I could, the Devil following, letting me guide him. I pushed through a couple in our way; we were almost in the main room. The heat had folded, rounding around the contour of my shoulder. It was approaching my neck and breasts, my knees were weak, but I kept going. We made it out of the room. By the time I reached the back door, I was moaning. I forced my eyes back open. People were staring, smiling. Some guy fist-pumped the air. But I wasn't able to care; the heat was overwhelming. My hands trembled as I twisted the doorknob to the stairway. I barely made it up the first few steps on the stairs, crawled up them in a tangle, while ripping his shirt open, unbuckling his belt. Somehow, we made it to the darkness.

It was pure sensation, but also fully embodied. I was my body and his body. And a garden, honey, heat, sweetness, stars, and cosmic dust. Earth, as in dirt and as in the whole planet. I was spring, and the snakes in my veins were green. When they traveled up to my chest, they eased their purple-coiled sister, hardened around my heart, who slowly loosened and let go and turned green too. They swam in golden water and became gold; they swam in lava, then champagne, where they became air and effervesced, bubbling together, erupting into the air and leaving behind the surface of a lake at sunset, where I floated, bruised but free.

It is hard for me to fully understand it now. It was all immediate, all feeling; I could only understand it while I was feeling it. A little like the pain I had for Michael. I take my word for it that it was a real thing. I wish I could say it didn't hurt after that. It did. And after Michael, it happened again. The Devil had been right about my wanting what I couldn't have. But at least from then on, I knew myself. And eventually, it didn't hurt. And eventually, I learned.

At the party, the Devil had asked what was so special about Michael. Today the Devil and I would shake our heads at that young version of me, like the frustrated parents of a teenager. Immersed in the present, it can be hard to know where to look. Sometimes you need the distance to fully appreciate the view, to see mountaintops surrounding the creek and know that if you had kept going farther to the left, you would have seen a canyon so vast, it is hard to believe you missed it. You can see it all together from afar, even though by then, the sound of the water, the mist, and the soft moss are gone.

I saw the Devil twice after that, but he didn't see me. The first time, much later, at a bar. The Devil was wearing a dark forest green shirt that suited him perfectly, telling a beautiful blond about a decade younger than me something hilarious. There was no jealousy. Seeing him like that made me happy. I looked away for a couple of seconds as a man squeezed next to me at the bar to order a drink, and when I looked back, the Devil and his girl were gone. The man who had squeezed in turned out to be Peter, who later became my husband.

Michael and Angela broke up in the summer of 1983. Our friendship had cooled a little by then, fizzling out until we lost touch at the end of the eighties. About a year ago, she found me on social media. It was so strange to see her profile picture, to recognize her features within that aged face. It was hard to understand it, not having experienced it gradually as I did with my own. I tried to picture my face today and subtract from it my face when she'd known me. It was hard to see either one with any precision.

Later, Angela DMed a scan of a photograph of the two of us together that Halloween, as Nancy and Diana. We were beautiful and had that puppy quality, that youth-soaked snout. I wished I could explain to myself in 1981, and myself now, how time worked. Its mind-boggling speed, even when each day can be slow like a trudge through tar. How you blink, and here you are. How those silly nights feel like some freaky moving Escher picture of a mountain peak appearing to get smaller and smaller in the rearview mirror, but somehow still there in its full size. I ended up unfriending and blocking Angela a couple of months later. She turned out to be one of the 52 percent. She was ecstatic about the election. It was too much for me to witness.

The second time I saw the Devil was at the inauguration. Peter was in the shower. I absentmindedly turned on the TV; we had no interest in watching it. I was about to turn it off when I saw him. The camera moved from a close-up to a wider shot, and he was there, next to a red-haired woman, three rows behind the podium. He had not aged. He frowned slightly, a serious, focused expression. He looked at his watch. The camera cut to a tighter shot of the inauguration ceremony, and he was gone.

{　}

The writer wasn't sure if she had ever been in love with the Devil. He could have made it so, she supposed, but that would have been unlike him. In the beginning, not long after they met, she was lining up at the bodega and wondered if the Devil was going to proposition her—for her soul, that is. The Devil answered, suddenly standing behind her in line, holding a six-pack and a newspaper, that she could keep her soul to herself. The writer paid for her purchase and stepped aside. She apologized for being presumptuous. She had heard stories. The Devil raised an eyebrow as he handed the cashier a bill. He let him keep the change and turned toward her. Her soul was hers to do what she liked; he wished he could say the same about himself. He couldn't have her whole soul. But maybe she could tell him more of her story. And she did, willingly, walking back home as the sun set, late that summer night. It wasn't much that time, but he listened and understood her, and it felt like a kind of love.

Years later, Peter and the writer went to the Met together. They were at an exhibition when Peter had to take a call from work. He left her standing by Cézanne's *Mont Sainte-Victoire and the Viaduct of the Arc River Valley*. As she looked at the painting, the

Devil showed her how to find herself in it. Not the central tree interrupting the view or any of the others in the foreground. She wasn't the tranquil green landscape in the background, the valley, the mountains, the bridge. She was a brushstroke. The Devil traced her through a yellowing-green section of the grassy fields. Here was her birth, where the brush first touched the canvas, a minute movement to the right, her as a young child grabbing the spider, bringing it to her mouth, her mother wrapping her in a blanket and lifting her, the car ride to the ER, her throat swelling with venom. The Devil followed the grooves of the brushstroke, and she hid behind the brown sofa in her aunt's library, waited for the sound of the door closing, and stood, ran her fingers on the red leather-bound covers. Here was the chalk breaking on the blackboard when she was called to write her answers. Here she was with that boy, in the stairway to the basement of her building, his lips on her neck, the first time anyone's lips met her like that. Here was the long bus ride in the dark. Here was being caught in the rain, her socks and her hair soaked, her shirt stuck to her body, her kicking a puddle for the splash; here, her mother and aunts together peeling tiny shrimp for the bobó, caruru, and vatapá; here, her pinching out a chunk of cotton candy. A slight turn of the brush, her taking Peter's hand, leading him to that dark part of the garden at his friend's wedding reception. Here, the nights staring at her clock, the steady filling of notebooks. Packing the apartment, quitting her job, and leaving the office at 10:30 A.M. The man cooking at the halal cart, people rushing to Penn Station, Midtown moving as it always did as she walked away from it, into the lake at sunset, the orange water, cold crossing her belly button, her chest, dunking her head in, the silver-speckled darkness of the water mixing with the sky as night fell.

The Devil skipped to another section of the painting, where the grass met a curving path. He said he liked how the aquamarine turned into a dark forest green, right there, he pointed and smiled. He turned his gaze away from the painting, toward the entrance to the gallery. Peter walked in. The Devil disappeared.

# GHOST STORY

I was writing this story about a man who invented elaborate lies to seduce each of his three roommates. To the first woman, he made a confession, walking on Fifth Avenue on their way back to the subway from his special gelato place, his private place he had not shared with anyone until that day, when he brought her. He told her he was a trust fund baby who rejected all the money from his coldhearted parents because it was important for him to prove to them and, most importantly, to himself that he could make it on his own. To the second roommate, he said, wiping his eyes, then hers after the two of them watched *All about My Mother* on Netflix, that he'd been abandoned by his drug-addicted mother, who in turn had been abandoned by her mother, in a tragic unbreakable cycle. Heartbroken since infancy, he said, irresistibly, he'd never been able to fully let himself trust anyone. To the third roommate, he whispered one evening over takeout, after the cat suddenly jumped on the piano keys, that his lineage was cursed and that the ghost of a distant relative's lover haunted his inherited piano. Seeing her eyes widen, he put his chopsticks down and took her hand to his chest, asking her to feel his heartbeat.

My Saturday-morning writing group read a draft, but none of them saw the protagonist as a trickster. They believed his stories were true, at least within the text. When I got back to my apartment after meeting them, damp from the thin mixture of rain and snow that followed me across the Manhattan Bridge back to Brooklyn, I called my mother in Brazil:

"So I have this story I'm writing. A guy tells one of the girls he lives with that his parents are loaded."

"Hm."

"He tells his other roommate that he was abandoned by his mother." I sat down on my gray Ikea couch. "And the third woman, about a ghost haunting him."

"How many women are there?" my mother asked. "Why do they live with him?"

"Well, rent is expensive, etcetera. The usual reasons." I balanced the phone between my shoulder and ear and removed my wet socks.

"Why live with strangers? Don't they have families?"

"Mom." I suddenly felt tired. "Come on."

"OK, some guy lies to girls stupid enough to live with strange men they find on the internet. What's new? Sharing an apartment with people you don't know cannot end well."

"Mom, if you met Marc, you'd love him. There's nothing to worry about." I held my glasses, still foggy, covered with tiny drops of water, and wiped each lens with the edge of my scarf. The world went blurry for those seconds and became clear again as I put my glasses back on. "But, yes, exactly: The stories my protagonist tells the women are made up."

"Ué, of course, they are. I thought sharing a place was just for when you were going to college."

The weak diffuse light entering my small living room made it look like it was late afternoon. But the alarm clock on our one exposed brick wall insisted there were two minutes to midday.

"Well, Mom. I don't do it because I want to."

"OK, OK. Do you have to live with this guy, though? I mean, have you seen the pictures he posts? The parties?"

"Pictures? Where?"

"I friended him, about a month ago."

"Mom, you have to stop doing that."

"What if he was a psycho? A Trump supporter?"

"Meu Deus. He's not a Trump supporter! Plus, you know what the equivalent of a Trump supporter in Brazil is?"

"Oh, let's not go there again. You left too long ago to know what it's like: the corruption! The violence!"

I almost pointed out, again, that she was just repeating words from TV and social media clips verbatim. Or asked what she meant exactly, based on what, etc., again. But I knew it wouldn't go anywhere, like the many other times we'd tried to talk about the situation in Brazil before. My mother, who was quiet now, must've felt the same way. I felt the browning edge of a leaf of my baby ficus plant on the coffee table. I drew a tiny spiral in the soil with my finger. It was dry. I walked to the sink, grabbed a half-filled glass of water, and poured it into the pot then went back to my story. "So my character, the guy sharing the apartment with the three women: People get confused thinking all his lies are true. They get tricked by him."

"If these friends of yours visited here, they'd be like dodos, falling for any scheme that waltzed their way." She perked up, her voice excited. "Oh, did you know someone called last week pretending to have kidnapped you?"

"Me?" I looked down at my bare feet on the worn wooden floor.

"Yes, they go, 'We have your daughter,' and put on some woman crying in the background: 'Mom, Mom,' etcetera."

It was such a well-known cliché of a scheme, the "we have your child" call. But I found myself wanting something, some reaction from my mother. "What did you do?" I asked, trying to sound casual.

"I asked them, 'Where did you find her, this daughter of mine? Tell her I sit here waiting for her. Every day, I wait and wait, but she never comes.'"

Birds chirped on my mother's end of the line. Outside my apartment, the trees were dry naked twigs. I didn't know if my mother had really said that to the scammers or just wanted to say it to me now.

"I don't think anyone heard anything," she continued. "It was such a ruckus, uma bagunça danada, the girl in the background with this loud fake weeping. You know the kind that is interested in declaring itself as weeping? Like you and your brother, when you were children. I told the guy, 'Tell her to quit being so ungrateful and give her old mother a call.'"

"Mom, I call you all the time."

"Yeah, yeah, but I thought that was what a mom type would do. I could've spelled it out for them: 'You could not have kidnapped my daughter, for she has left us for America.'" She stirred a drink, the spoon hitting the edge of the cup, tiny clinks with each turn. "But then I would be asking them to kidnap one of us for real. They think you go to America and you're loaded. Ha!" She paused for a sip.

"Weren't you scared?" I wondered how she would have felt if the fake-kidnapping victim had been my brother, Miguel, instead of me, but I dropped the question as soon as it took form.

"Nah. Everyone was home. Your father was on the couch, your brother also, right next to Juliana. And you—well. All I had to do was count the people watching the soap opera, and I knew the guy was full of it. Anyway, I put him on speaker. Your brother was laughing. Then he got up with his phone and started recording the whole thing. The video is doing the rounds. Wanna hear it? Wait a second." Before I could reply, she put the phone down and shouted after my brother in the background ("Ô, Miguel, help me out over here, come find the clip"), TV voices faintly accompanying hers. She came back to the line. "He's in the shower. You can search the hashtag, something like #sequestra doretiazinha or #tiadosequestro. Oh, I don't remember. Your brother will send it to you later. Anyway, why don't you stop this roommate nonsense and come back to live with us?"

At least it wasn't just me who saw through my character's lies. But later I checked with two more of my friends. They both thought the stories the man told his roommates were true too. And my mother, the only person on my team, had not even read the story, written in English. In the end, I changed it to fit the prevalent reading. And I did that by changing nothing. No edits to the words printed on the hibiscus tea–stained manuscript. The change happened only in my mind. For a moment, I wished the change would have happened in the readers' minds instead, but it seemed clear by now that I was only wishing for what I couldn't have. So I decided that yes, now all the stories the guy told were true, including the ghost one, in fiction I'd initially thought was a little far-fetched but still realistic. And that was the end of the question, at least for now.

A few weeks later, my mother called me:

"You need to do something about this ghost."

"Ghost?" I opened and closed the kitchen drawer where I usually left my keys. I was late to work.

"Yeah, ghost."

"Mom, what are you talking about? We believe in ghosts now?" Not on the table or the counter. Marc must have taken them by mistake, again.

"Whether you believe it or not doesn't matter. It's here, haunting me."

I didn't understand why she was suddenly talking about ghosts. Was she leading us into some sort of metaphor? I couldn't see how to interpret it. The microwave blinked 8:13. I had a meeting. I had to get to work right away.

"What are you trying to say, Mom?" Maybe she really thought she had seen a ghost? Was that possible? "Are you feeling okay? Maybe put on Dad or Miguel?"

"I'm fine. And no, I can't put them on. Your father is out, and your brother"—she sighed—"is traveling with Juliana again. They're talking about having the wedding in Minas Gerais instead of here. Can you believe it? Those people of hers." She sucked her teeth. "Well, even if he were here, you'd have to help me with this one. Not him."

"Why?"

"Because this ghost is yours."

"What do you mean 'mine'? It's not like I have a stash of ghosts to send out like postcards." I sounded incredulous without meaning to. I didn't know what to think. If I could only find my keys.

"I mean"—her voice wavered—"it's you."

I stopped looking for my keys. My mom sounded genuinely concerned. Something was truly bothering her. I worried about her more and more. Her getting older added another layer of complications to living so far away.

"But I'm here, Mom." I tried to project something, reassurance maybe, like a parent hushing a child who had awakened from nightmares. I hoped she could really hear me. That I could make her feel better and make this scary ghost talk go away. And even without knowing the exact shape of my fear for her, I felt it, constricting my throat and stomach. I wondered what she looked like at that moment on the other side. I thought I could just hear her breathing, but I wasn't sure. "I'm right here."

"If I were going crazy," she said slowly, as if trying to persuade a child of something she couldn't quite understand, "I'd probably just see a regular ghost—say, your grandmother, or maybe a great-grandparent, or an old-fashioned count with an ill-timed real estate ambition. Something predictable like that. But it's you. You are older, but it's still you. I don't have the imagination for this kind of nonsense."

She had a point. She sounded like she was reasoning properly. Except for the whole ghost part. What was happening to her? Whatever it was, I wished it would disappear. That my mom would reveal it was all a misunderstanding or a joke. But she sounded so serious, so worried.

"But I'm alive," I said gently, "talking to you right now."

"You say"—she paused—"the ghost says she comes from the future."

"The future?"

"When are you coming home, Filha?"

When I hung up the phone, I thought again about my plans to go somewhere else, anywhere, for my vacation this year. I imagined myself walking down the cobblestones in Lisbon, passing by graffitied walls in Berlin, parallel universes I would never access. I always ended up going back to Brazil. With my brother's engagement and now my mom's ghost thing, I let my tourist other selves disappear in a little puff of blue smoke. In the reality of my apartment, I saw my keys on the couch, glinting in the sunlight.

The plane landed in Brasília close to noon. I passed through the sliding glass doors, squinting at the blinding brightness that marked my visits. The light, permeating everything along with the dry heat, always made my first days back feel otherworldly. Far away, past the parking lots, lay the short patch of grass, the sparse savanna, the few short twisted trees of the Cerrado. The sky was everywhere, over and in between buildings, touching the red dirt on the horizon. I stood holding my hand like a visor. Arms embraced me: my mom and, when she finished with the first round, my dad.

When I first saw them, I was startled by my father's sunken cheeks, his scalp almost naked, save a thin spread of bluish-gray hair. My mother's papery skin, her softening neck. They were still in their midsixties but looked so much older than the image I carried with me in the US. The changes felt more dramatic with each visit, so striking to me, having missed the gradual recording of time on their faces, the invisible pace of the everyday. But this happened every time I came back, and I knew that within a few minutes, I would start to habituate to their present selves and not notice it anymore.

My mother also seemed shocked when she first looked at me. She kept mentioning how I looked so well, so young. That was not her style. She should have been asking me about the flight, complaining about Juliana's parents, or frantically looking for her keys, always lost in her large handbag. I looked at my father quizzically. He replied with a small shrug.

But as we walked to the parking lot, still side hugging, she seemed to be getting back to normal, except for the occasional stare and a pause to kiss my right cheek again, as if to confirm I was really there. The car was at the very edge of the lot.

"Your brother took the other car to Minas Gerais," my mother said, looking for her keys in her bag.

Minas Gerais was a full day's drive away, and they were with Juliana's family, which I knew bothered my mother. I was surprised to feel annoyed at that now. Maybe because I liked Juliana and wanted to defend her? No, not that. If were honest with myself, it was that, at least for that moment, I wanted me to be enough.

"Why didn't he take this car? It's only the two of them, no?"

"It's not a problem. We don't need it," my father yelled from behind the car, where he was loading the luggage into the trunk.

"Careful, or he will donate it to the church," I said.

None of us used to go to any church, but as a teenager, my brother announced out of the blue that he was joining a local evangelical youth group. He'd wanted to donate his car, an old Volkswagen Beetle, to them. Fortunately, he'd been a minor, and my parents would not let him. Now, more than a decade later, he'd graduated to convincing others to donate to the church instead. He was good at it, pleasant, relaxed, attentive. And he knew what people wanted to hear, whether it was about charity, "family values," or the fear of the end of the world. I loved him and had always resented him a little, for being so likable. But now there was more; it wasn't just about everyone liking him. They also believed him. I thought about my character in the story, his roommates in love with him. Did my brother really believe all he spouted?

"Don't pick at your brother," my mother said. "Here, hold this." She handed me some of the contents of her bag to make the search easier: a few documents, a hairbrush, and the squashed chocolates she still carried in case my brother or I got hungry. "They are all coming for dinner in a few days—her parents too."

That explained why my mother had called me a few weeks before the trip and asked me to bring a serving dish (instead of the usual perfume for her coworker's cousin or electronics for the neighbor's nephew's girlfriend or whoever it was; I couldn't keep track). Never mind that I grabbed her dish from the cheap seasonal items displayed by the entrance of Target. She would be proud of it and mention I brought it with me from the US. She had probably been thinking about this dinner for a while, at least since the call, and I was glad she had something to distract her from ghosts.

Across the parking lot, the airport looked small, flattened by all that sky. It had seemed tall up close, much more built up than it used to be when I first started traveling back from the US. Now the ceiling hovered far above, with enough room for three or four additional floors between it and the ground. Its recent renovation nodded to Brasília's original architecture: a white curving concrete pillar here, a modernist sculpture there, the occasional wall covered with the colorful geometric tiles of Athos Bulcão. A natural growth of the original core of the city, futuristic for the 1960s, but fused with a more recent architectural sense of the future. More metal, more glass, more open space, more light. But to me, even this futuristic architecture was becoming a fossil of the recent past. Too ominous, large and corporate, and, paradoxically, too optimistic to have anything to do with the future.

My parents started arguing about my mother having misplaced the keys. And while they argued about that, they developed a secondary argument on what route to take back home.

I turned around and faced a gap in the chain-link fence around the parking lot, a section of three or four panels missing that had probably just rusted off, given how deteriorated the fence looked. I took a couple of steps forward, toward the horizon, then a few more until I was just past the gap. When I shifted my gaze, nothing changed in the landscape. Because there were no mountains, hills, or tall buildings, if I tried to get closer or look at things from another angle, my perspective always stayed the same. Just a flat line, just as far away. I felt again as I sometimes did when I returned home: as if I had entered a dream. I looked at my hands to remind myself of my physical form. There they were, still holding my mom's things.

"Where are you going, menina? Come. I found the keys; now I have to look through that stuff" — she pointed to my hands — "to find the parking card."

\*　\*　\*

The last time I'd seen the house, it had been just a concrete skeleton; the structure had been there, but there had been no windows, doors, roof, or outer layers of smoothed concrete: a ruin in reverse. Now it was finally finished. And it was beautiful. I had expected it to be nice, but not this: a gorgeous modernist two-story house. It was hard to believe it was real, it was ours. Inside was a tall open square of air and light bracketed by plain bright white walls. The floor was covered by large smooth porcelain tiles, with the look of polished concrete but shinier, making them seem like water reflecting the windows. I wanted to touch its surfaces. The floor, the unadorned white walls. And the light everywhere. It came in through the windows, beams of sunlight, and it bounced, filling the house. Soft diffused light on the white sofa and our skin and hair. It was as if I were breathing it, that light. It was cool inside, no air-conditioning needed, despite the scorching afternoon. A solid concrete house. I was never comfortable in the wooden houses in the US, precarious and prone to burning. I understood then I'd been craving to live in concrete again. Within five minutes of being in my parents' new house, I wanted it to be mine because I felt as if I belonged to it. I began fantasizing about one day saving enough to buy it from them and have them live in it. A gift for them and for me.

It was clear from her satisfaction in giving me the tour, the way her gaze followed its lines, the open space, that my mother loved it too, despite her belief that her brand-new house was haunted. My mother and I had the same taste in most things. We hated knickknacks and clutter. We liked the unapologetic angles and openness in modernist architecture and suffered from a nostalgia for its past imagination of the future.

We went to the guest room on the second floor and stepped out onto a balcony. I knew she was proud of the nice view of the lake over the other concrete houses in the neighborhood, and I praised it, which

I could tell made her happy. But after a while, her face grew worried. She walked back into the room, and I followed her. Everything inside was temporarily dark as my eyes adjusted.

"This is my last house." She fluffed the pillows on the double bed. "I am not going to let a ghost, especially a ghost of someone who's not even dead, spoil it."

She didn't seem angry, but her expression was grave. It was as if she were warning me or the ghost, or both of us. I couldn't tell, and maybe she couldn't either. I wanted to comfort her but didn't know what to say. As I was growing up, it had been common for my aunts and many people we knew to believe in all sorts of things—auras, crystals, past lives, and spirits. Not fanatically so, but on a just-in-case basis. My mom had always humored her sisters and her friends, but she'd never seemed truly interested herself. I wasn't sure what was behind this ghost thing now, and I was scared for her, for where this was going. And for me. I needed her to be OK, as she had been just a few months before. I wasn't quite ready to believe the gravity of what was happening. I was waiting to find some rational explanation for why she was talking about ghosts that didn't involve her beginning to lose grasp of reality. Before I could say anything, she left me to go finish preparing dinner in the outside kitchen they'd built on the verandah.

At dinner, we sat out there, on that same verandah. A cricket was chirping in the dark backyard. My plate was set up for me already, the onioned beef, with tiny crunchy slivers of dried meat, yucca flour, rice, beans, and vinaigrette, pleasantly arranged. The smell, meat, butter, vinegar. It was as if a picture in a coffee table cookbook had fully come to life.

I stole a delicious bite of farofa soaked with vinaigrette, even though we were still waiting for my father, who was in the shower.

She updated me on the wedding plans. Yes, it would take place in

Minas Gerais. But the date was not set, "and venues book up; things change." She smiled. But at least they gave her the engagement party, which she would host here, in her new house. They would be discussing the wedding details when Miguel, Juliana, and her parents came for dinner in a couple of days. "I'll make sure the dinner is good and the party is very chique. You never know. Maybe they'll change their mind about having the wedding over there."

I nodded, my mouth full, vinaigrette-soaked yucca still melting on my tongue.

"Can I make you anything else? You are so skinny. You look so skinny and so young."

"Thanks?" I said, finishing my stolen bite.

"I guess I got used to looking at you older?"

"Huh? Oh, that."

"Never mind. Maybe she'll show up for you one day."

"What does Dad say about all this?"

"Ask him later. He promised to be quick to shower. He got a new polo at Carrefour to wear at dinner with you. Now he's taking forever, probably can't help but steal some glances at the novela. Ô, velho," she yelled out, "a menina 'tá com fome!"

We both giggled. In his old age, he had become addicted to the 9 P.M. soap operas (still referred to as the "8 P.M. novelas," because of their original scheduling several decades ago). Though he never admitted it, saying he liked having them as a background to his naps. To be fair, at least 50 percent of the time, when I walked past him in front of the TV, he was sleeping. How I missed him, without always realizing it. And now he was so close to me for real. He would be down from his shower anytime now.

"Anyway, it's very unfair," my mother continued. "No parent is perfect. You will learn that, once you have your own . . ." She stopped herself and swallowed, her eyes traveling up and slightly to the right, as if she remembered something, something sad. "Anyway, we tried our best. I did everything for you two, but I wasn't perfect. It's the same for your father. But she only haunts me."

Just then, there was a loud bang behind the kitchen counter. I jumped in my seat. The cricket stopped chirping.

My mother got up and ran to stand just behind the counter. "Shh-hhhh, shhhhhhh, shhhhhhhh." She waved her arms up and down. "Shhhhhhhh."

She stopped for a second. I could hear the TV commercials ("After your novela, stay tuned for *Big Brother Brasil*"). The cricket had not returned yet. My dad stopped at the door, looking at my mom, waiting.

Another noise in the kitchen. This time my dad joined in, both going, "Shhhhhhhh, shhhhhhhhhhhhhh," flailing their arms like birds.

That was it, I thought, both parents had gone insane.

Something dark and furry ran out of the kitchen. They relaxed.

"What's for dinner?" My father lifted the lid of a pot on the stove.

"What was that?" I asked.

"What? Oh, that was just the neighbor's cat. It found a way to get out again." My dad shrugged. "She said she'd take care of it. Yet here it is again."

The cricket was chirping again.

"Don't worry." My mom brought me a glass of guava juice. "She likes to come during the day."

"What kind of ghost is that?"

She raised her eyebrows, tilted her head to the side. "She says she misses the light."

I shivered. Was there no light where she was coming from? I tried to tell myself again that there was no ghost, to convince myself the whole thing was nonsense, as I ran my hands over the goose bumps on my arms.

After breakfast the next day, I sat at the outdoor dining table, looking through the feedback I had received from the writing group on another of my stories. They asked for more details on the father character, who was not by any means my father. But my dad was gardening right in the yard, possibly making sure everything was in order for the dinner, at my mom's request. So now I began to write about the father gardening without gloves, red dirt covering his hands, stuck under his fingernails. Yes, the dirty red hands suited the story. My dad lifted his hat and wiped his brow. It was a legionnaire hat I'd brought him from the US last time. I knew he hated sunscreen, which I made him wear when I was around. But most of the time, I wasn't here. I'd thought he would find the hat cool. "Like an explorer in the desert," he'd said when I'd given it to him. But it had been suspiciously clean until now, when he took it off, leaving red finger marks in the otherwise-pristine khaki fabric. He'd worn it today just for me. He looked at me and waved—a sweet, goofy smile. In the story, I made it a red baseball cap and made the father's appearance menacing. The writing group had also said nothing much happened in the story. Which was true.

I needed to take a break.

I got a cup of coffee in the kitchen. My dad came in holding three yucca roots. "For lunch," he said proudly.

"So, what's with Mom and the ghost thing?"

He put the yuccas in the sink and looked at the garden. "You know, I—I mean, we, your mother included—are not the type to be talking about witches, ghosts, and fairies. You know that. She never brought up something like this before. Now, have I seen any ghosts? Ever? No.

I don't believe in ghosts. But I believe your mother. So that's that."
He turned on the sink to wash his hands. "At the very least, it is true
to her. And I respect that."

"Easy for you to say." I sipped my coffee. "It's not your ghost."

He put his arm around my shoulder. "I know. But be patient with
her. The ghost has been hard on her lately."

"But you don't believe in ghosts."

"I don't know. You have always been too sure of things, how things
are, how things work. Even more so since you left."

"Because I don't believe that I am a ghost?"

"No, not just that. What is happening there, what is happening
here . . ."

"That man is the Devil, Dad. How can anyone in their right mind
vote for him?"

"Yeah, he is far from our first choice. But the Workers' Party has
been a disgrace for this country."

"Who said anything about the Workers' Party? What about everyone else? You're beginning to sound like Miguel."

"See?" He tilted his head slightly as if pointing at me.

I took a deep breath and sat back down in front of my laptop.
When my brother had first joined his church, my parents had been as
unhappy as I was. It was the kind of church that constantly asked for
money, despite the Audis and BMWs that always carried the pastors,
CEO types who had found the Lord only after getting their MBAs
overseas. Miguel was not stupid. It was baffling to us that he didn't see
this. And the church required his presence too much; once he joined,
he was never home anymore. Instead, he went to services between five
to seven times a week. But over the years, with me living overseas and
him living right here with them, me combative and him always pleasant, he began gaining ground. Now I was the weird one in the family.

Although my parents never joined the church, they no longer criticized it, not even the fact its high-ranking pastors were getting too cozy with politicians or running for office themselves, with the full and blind support of their congregations. The previous year when I was back here on vacation, I found their car, the nice one that my brother liked to borrow, with a campaign sticker for one of the deputados pushed by the church. His platform included a pledge to end "gender philosophy" and return to "family values." The conversation had begun okay. They were just humoring my brother, they had said, then: "We don't agree with the guy on everything, but he goes to your brother's church. I mean, Miguel knows him. And that Workers' Party . . ." It had ended with a big ugly fight close to the end of my last day. I knew that talking further now was useless.

"What's Miguel's take? I mean, what does he say about the ghost?" I asked my father now.

"He listens to her." My father finished washing the dirt off the last yucca and left it to dry on the dish rack. "Tells her he knows what it's like to know something is true, even when others might not believe you. Talks about faith. It works. Makes her feel better about the whole thing."

Of course, Miguel went along with her, and, of course, they loved it. I almost said that out loud but kept it in. I knew it was no use.

"I don't know, Filha." My father placed a glass of water on the table next to me. "The older I get, the less sure I am of anything." He kissed the top of my head and went inside.

I stayed in the same spot at the table outside, but after staring at the screen for a while, I stopped working on the father story. A light rain began, stirring up a smell of rain and earth, the red dirt where my father had been working turning a shade darker with each drop. I opened the roommate story. It was now a ghost story, I reminded myself. I typed "Ghost Story" at the top of the page and wondered where to start. Maybe trying to inhabit the ghost, to understand it better. This ghost, who hadn't been there in the first place, who'd snuck in there without my knowing. In the story, the ghost had been stuck in a piano. I thought of its vaporous spirit, a vaguely human-shaped blue smoke, squeezing under the lid into the wooden case, undulating between the strings, silently running its steam fingers through the hammers, circling the inner walls of the case, so similar to the walls of its coffin, and curling itself, lying on the key bed, like a sleeping cat. Until someone came in to play a song, a tribute to the ghost's former self, jolting it awake, beating at it with the hammers, making its smoky body dissipate and sink into the fibers of the wood, the ivory keys, until it merged with them. And the player's fingers touched the ghost as they played the song. And it was so nice to feel touch again. And it was as if the ghost were playing the music too.

It wasn't working. I swayed on my chair, pushed it back away from the table a few inches, and tried again. I closed my eyes and imagined myself as the ghost, not seeing it from the outside this time. I imagined looking down at my fingers. There were my mother's white-tiled verandah floors through the faint blue smoke that was me. I brought my hands to my face, silently, I had no mouth. And my body was not constant; I had to think of its shape, its limits, or it would disappear. Grasping for the human form, I thought of the statues, *Os Candangos*, the two figures at Praça dos Três Poderes, and I was there. I was able to keep close to a human shape, as one of them. I was made of bronze and eight meters tall. But then the two spirits who lived there already asked without saying anything, as the hole in their heads was neither eye nor mouth, what I was doing there. Before I could reply, they continued, reminding me that the sculpture had been a gift to them, named after them, in exchange for their bodies, which remained to this day trapped in concrete at the base of a lecture hall, the education auditorium, at the then-new university and, unless I was planning to bring them back, could I, kindly, remove myself from their statues. I had to leave. So I went then to the only place I knew I could go: my parents' house. I tried to find an outline for myself again and couldn't. I was thinning out into nothing. Until my mom went to the bathroom to wash her hands and looked at herself in the mirror. And I felt a pull toward that shape, her face in the reflection, I fit myself into it, and the fit was right. I was so happy to have found an outline that I started to laugh. I lifted my hands to touch my face, an old woman's face, and it felt so good to feel something with my fingers again. Right then, I looked up and saw my mother, her hands on her cheeks, screaming.

"A bunch of thieves in the government. And all these criminals, these marginais, vagabundos, killing and raping. The country has never been worse," a man was yelling on TV.

I opened my eyes and closed my laptop, not having written a word.

"Back when the military was in power, no one would dare," he continued.

"Well, I must say, here we agree," a woman said. "Even if I, unlike Senhor Rodrigo here, think there were troubling incidents then, I keep thinking, what's worse? Having a curfew and watching what you say on TV, or fearing for your life every time you step out of the house?"

"When they kill your son, this bunch of marginais, when they rape your daughter, I want to see if you come to me speaking of human rights. These Workers' Party people, these red criminals, they only care about filling their coffers."

I felt nauseated. I covered my ears with my hands and walked toward the TV room.

"Dad, can you please turn this down?" I asked. But I found him sleeping on the sofa. I turned the TV off.

Dinner was a test run for the next day, when my brother would arrive and Juliana's family would join us. My mother was in a bad mood, stressed about impressing them. My dad, who was accustomed to her, stood up and grabbed his plate as soon as it was ready, claiming he couldn't wait for her delicious cooking and was going now to watch his novela. Mom and I ate the bobó in silence. Although she had cooked it for my brother, it was also my favorite dish, and tonight's bobó was especially good, the smell and taste of dendê infused in the yucca. But I didn't say anything. I knew my mother was probably not yet satisfied with dinner and missed Miguel. I didn't let myself admit it often, but I missed him too. The old Miguel, but even the new one, who was not so new anymore. I thought about his face as a child, the two of us racing and playing hide-and-seek at Praça dos Três Poderes, his round little kid cheeks, his mouth always open, following me around, asking, "Where are you going?" I missed him, even though I didn't understand who he was becoming.

My mom was stabbing at her food aggressively. I didn't want to fight. But it was getting to me.

"What's bugging you, Mom?"

"What's bugging me," she repeated flatly.

"Yes, what's bugging you?"

"Well, you." She huffed. "I mean, she won't give me a break."

The poor woman and her ghosts.

"What's she saying now?" I put an arm around her.

"Even knowing about Miguel, she can't give me a break." She closed her eyes, ran her hand over her forehead.

"You mean the wedding? Mom, Juliana is great, who cares if the wedding is in Minas Gerais? I bet you your party will be better than the wedding, especially if you make this bobó."

"No, it's not that. I forget what I tell each of you." She sighed. "They are planning to move away."

"Move away? To Minas Gerais?" No wonder she was unhappy.

"No. To Canada."

My poor mother. It was probably hard on her when I moved. But Miguel leaving her . . . this would nearly kill her.

"Oh, Mom. I'm so sorry."

She let go of my hand and stepped away. Her expression wasn't sad anymore but angry again.

"And your ghost said I prefer your brother." She looked at my face, searching for something. "The nerve of her, so ungrateful, after all that I have done for you." She paused as if waiting for me to say something, then continued. "After you left me." Her lips tightened. She looked toward the grass and the darkness, where the cricket chirped. "I have always treated you the same way."

She wanted me to contradict the ghost, to assure her I thought the ghost was lying. And I almost gave her what she wanted, but my throat closed up, and the words pushing against it made me feel sick. I couldn't do it. I felt it'd always been obvious to everyone that my mother preferred Miguel. But my mother had a delusion that no one noticed.

"And I think all her talk about the fires and the forest and the blue smoke is just a front."

"What fires, Mom?"

"She talks about all that stuff, but I think she's just angry because of the will."

"What will?"

"She must be angry because I'm leaving the house to your brother."

"What?"

"See?"

"See what? Why?"

"He was here when we built it, and he was going to be here. And we used to talk about his and Juliana's children ruining the paint job with crayons. Where were you?" Her voice faltered, but she gained control of it again, hardening her face further. "Also because he would never come back to haunt me over material possessions."

The thought of my mother's love for Miguel's unborn children made me remember her looking at him as a child. I wanted to go back in time and hold my child self, run my fingers through her hair. Love her. But the sadness of that thought and the fear of where it would take me made my limbs go limp as if I were losing my grip on my body, and I grabbed on to my anger instead. "Who says she's haunting you because of that?"

"Well, you appeared the night after I signed the will."

"After? You did this before she showed up? But then you can't have changed the will because of her."

"Why not?"

"Because the will came first."

"Talk to me after a ghost comes to haunt you, from the future, from after you're dead."

"You're dead?"

"Well, that's not exactly a spoiler. The ghost is old herself. It is not like I'm going to be around forever."

This was a thing my mother liked to bring up, not too often, but often enough so that it would be remembered. How I would realize things once she was gone, and by "realize," she meant "regret." I usually ignored her attempts to guilt me. But my mother looked so old right now. She would be gone one day, and I would have no one to come back to. And I would have chosen to spend all my time so far away.

I held her hand. "She told you that?"

"Yes."

"Oh. I'm so sorry, Mom." I hugged her. "Maybe she's just sad. Maybe she has nowhere to go. Or maybe she just misses you."

I thought about longing for my mom in the US and feeling her real self, not a disembodied voice on the phone, her body as I hugged her now. It was so easy and so hard to be with her. I had her with me now, and now was all I could be sure about. That terrified me.

"The thing that gets to me is that she is not angry when she says these things," she said, letting herself lean into my embrace for a moment. "She says the house doesn't matter. She says so many things we think matter don't. She tells me she's glad I am gone."

I gasped. "Mom, that's horrible. I would never say that."

"No, she says it kindly. She says things are not easy for those who survived and that I did a fine job as a mother. That it's okay to have some regrets. But that those who are still around have regrets of a magnitude we can't yet comprehend."

I held her hand, to comfort both of us. This ghost, I reminded myself, was nothing—could be nothing—but my mother's imagination. Her guilt, maybe. I was worried. But worried about her, I told myself. And me living far away while this, whatever it was, was happening to her. How things would change over here, how she, an old woman seeing ghosts, would manage, now and in a few years. And my fear for her here mixed with my fear for myself in the US. I told myself to focus. This was not some postapocalyptic story. This was my mother.

But still, I asked, because I had to, "Did you actually change the will before the ghost appeared?"

She got up and took our plates to the sink, her lips tight, her nose raised in disgust. She grabbed a cloth hanging on the kitchen faucet and started wiping the counter. "This is my house. I do with it what I want."

The ghost was right. It was not the house that mattered. But something else here did.

She kept wiping, looking down at the black counter. "You didn't want anything to do with this place. What do you want a house for? You left us"—she paused for a few seconds and began wiping again—"first."

The counter reflected part of her arm. The rest of her disappeared into the stone's darkness, making it look like a phantom limb following her movements under the surface, my mother and her ghost, cleaning the counter from both sides.

I was about to cry, and I didn't want her to see me this way. I went to the bathroom and cried quietly, hearing the muffled sounds from my dad's dubbed American movie, and, in the moments when the movie went quieter, my mother clearing the kitchen. I removed my glasses, and I wiped my eyes, washed my face and hands in cold water. Then, for a second, I thought I felt her, the ghost. It was as if she were there with me. I looked up at the mirror and saw a blurry version of my face, our face, mine, my mother's, the ghost's. We were all so sad. I cupped my cheek with one hand and touched the mirror with the other, our eyes, out of focus, met. I wanted to take the ghost with me, for my mother's sake and for the ghost's, so that she had somewhere to go, where she was welcome. But I put my glasses back on, and she was gone. I ripped a piece of paper towel and wiped my fingerprints from the mirror. I decided, when I got back home, I was going to revise that story. Make a clear decision on the ghost: one way or another.

{ }

The writer was on a darkened plane on her way back home to
Brazil, her first trip back with Peter. The writer and Peter had
wanted to synchronize their screens to watch a movie together,
but after a few tries, they gave up on getting it right and allowed
for a small asynchrony: his screen slightly ahead of hers, giving
her the impression that the position of his body, the slight fluctu-
ations of his breathing, the tension of his hold of her hand were a
way to predict what was coming. She had a hard time focusing on
the plot and ended up taking her headphones off. She watched
him watch the on-screen couple in her near future making angels
in the snow, a scene designed to move Americans, like amber-lit
rooms filled with people sipping cider on Thanksgiving or freshly
baked human-shaped cookies. Things that reminded Americans
of childhood and family, and reminded her of television reruns. It
was difficult to imagine Peter in Brasília then. She could picture
the two of them in Rio or São Paulo, places she had only visited
once, where both of them would be tourists. But not in the thick
shade of the Brasília ipês, shouting to be heard over cicadas and
walking on sidewalks cracked and stained so that it was difficult
to tell where the concrete finished and the red dirt began. She

had felt excited to show him where she came from, but when they talked about the places they would visit, the Palace of Dawn, the Esplanade, the Ermida, she sounded like an unfinished Wikipedia page. She didn't know how to put what she wanted him to know into words.

It was also her first time back since she had met the Devil. When the writer was a child, she had seen the face of the Devil as the woodcut-stamped horned figure in the folk prints and pamphlets of Brazilian cordel or as Darkness in the movie *Legend*. She knew his many names: "Bad Thing," "The Horned One," "Diabo," "Belzebu," "Capeta," "Satanás." When she was a child, she had been playing with her cousins, building a little city with the pile of sand and broken terra-cotta bricks left over from the construction at her aunt's house, when her aunt overheard her cousin Mariana ask, "What the Devil is this?" Mariana had been mimicking the affected old-fashioned style of dubbed movies, which picked outdated expressions over bad words or slang that might be too edgy or ephemeral. Her aunt called them all to the door and warned them: "Each time you say his name, he will take one step closer to you. You must never say his name." The writer had been terrified and spent several days trying to estimate how many steps there were between her and the Devil.

Peter was now asleep. She loved the way his closed eyes, his neat thick eyebrows, his parted lips looked in the soft light from the movie. Her screen seemed to malfunction, lines running across it as if she were playing a bad VHS tape, then static, like *Poltergeist*, then the movie *Legend* was on. "All I wish is for you to sit and talk with me," Darkness said in a closed caption. She smiled and whispered, "Hi," and then, knowing the Devil would understand the mischief, whispered his many names. The Devil as Darkness smiled straight at her from the screen. The screen glitched again, and went dark for a second, and returned to the movie she'd been watching with Peter—the two screens now perfectly synchronized.

At the airport, her parents looked older, again. They loved Peter. She had finally met someone. She was finally going to stop living in strange roommate arrangements. Walking across the living room in the new house was like walking on water. The cream polished stone reflected the people on it in a twisted, topsy-turvy way. When they all left for the kitchen (to show Peter a real cashew, not the nut, but the fruit that hung from it), another presence was reflected on the ground. The Devil looked around the living room with a face that said, "Not bad." The Devil, who had been forever banished from home with nothing but a condemned soul, for reasons she couldn't quite make sense of, after trying Saint Augustine, Wikipedia, and even the Bible. The Devil looked at a photo of the writer's brother on the minimalist modern white bookshelves by the TV. Her brother wore a suit and received some sort of award on the stage of his corporate megachurch.

After lunch, they went out to buy local crafts from the markets around the TV tower. The writer's father wanted to take Peter to try açaí at a local stall, the savory dish the writer's dad had as a child, not the sugary stuff that was just starting to become fashionable in other parts of Brazil and would later spread to health-focused smoothie shops around the world. Hearing the writer's father talk to Peter, the Devil paused his browsing at a table of baroque-looking figurines to raise an eyebrow; he shook his head and nodded toward Peter. Following the Devil's warning, the writer walked toward them, but they were already off. She lost them, running into a small passing crowd of nuns in light-gray habits and schoolchildren on a field trip.

Later, Peter, not used to the local germs in the water mixed with the açaí berries, was homebound, sick for four days. While he rested, the writer walked the barbed wire perimeter of her parents' condominium. Vines snaked around the fence and flowered. When everyone napped after lunch, the Devil waited for her in the outdoor kitchen, having coffee and milk and a piece of cassava cake. She sat across from him, and he silently nudged her notebook in her direction. She wrote, and when she looked up, the Devil was gone, and she was the one drinking the coffee and eating the cake. Her father worked in the garden, his hands covered in red dirt. He'd dug up two cassava roots to show Peter. In the evening, her mom and dad told stories to Peter, about the writer as a child, about the Northeast. Peter listened. She caught a glimpse of the Devil hiding behind her in the mirror. He was listening too. When Peter was better, they flew to the Northeast, to Bahia, where she used to go every summer to stay with her aunt and cousins. At the bay, the sand was white, and the water was not blue or gray but sepia, a rusty brown from the sediments, or minerals, or from mixing with the river, or something like that. The color looked more beautiful than it should, though a little apocalyptic. At the beach, the roots of many of the palm trees were completely exposed, the soil having eroded around them, and yet they were miraculously still standing. It was almost the end of the year. On New Year's Day, there would be white roses dotting the shoreline, washed back along with other offerings sent to Iemanjá the night before. She wanted to show Peter, who was at the little colonial chapel up the hill with her parents. But there were no roses yet, and they would be back in the US before New Year's. The Devil appeared beside her. He could see the roses to come, the petals moving as water reached over them in the sand and receded. The Devil whispered to her about how nice the roses and the water were in the darkness of their return flight, and she liked hearing him talk. She turned off her screen and reached for her notebook and her pen.

Back in New York, the writer looked up lists of mid-century modern buildings in the city. She scrolled and scrolled. But the buildings didn't call for her. Except for one, the Guggenheim. She didn't like how obvious it felt, not a hidden gem by any means. But it had some of what she craved. So she got on the subway and went to revisit it.

She stood on the corner across from the museum. She felt the winter air on her forehead, but she was well covered otherwise: scarf over half her face, gloves, her hands in her pockets, the right socks. Her puffy jacket was optimized for utility rather than looks. She had learned well, to live here. She appreciated now, how New York winters were often sunny, the skies bright blue, as they were today. She liked the clarity of this crisp air, the angle of the sun in winter. It was as if an optometrist cleaned her lenses, the way she couldn't do herself: completely clear. A perfect day to see the building. She loved the exterior. That matte-white concrete could be a stylized picture in a postcard, textureless, blank. But also, that white concrete was a delicious contradiction of textures. It was paper, and the freshly painted walls of the apartments of her childhood, and the chalky white concrete of Brasília. The outside walls of the Brazilian Congress building, the cupula shaped like a round plate facing down, and its counterpart, a plate facing up, two halves of a circle, which she had touched. The Guggenheim looked as if someone had put together the two hemispheres of the congress together and molded the sphere into a cylinder, then peeled it like an orange. The writer had seen the building so many times but felt as if she were discovering feelings toward an old friend. This, she declared to herself, was also home. It was not the same, not Brasília, but maybe it shouldn't be. She was here now.

She didn't look at any art inside this time. She followed the spiral inside ramps of the building, how the curve guided her way, trajectory up, down. She thought of water swirling clockwise and anticlockwise, depending on the hemispheres. The museum was lively, as they often were in New York City, but it wasn't too crowded. She had arrived early enough for it to be just right. She loved the footsteps and the muffled echoes of conversations around her, that way things sounded in the large space of a museum like this. She loved the people in awe, like her, and the people who didn't really notice, looking at their phones as they walked. The two children who ran down, dodging the crowd in a path that made it look like they were in a pinball machine. She loved how the building literally moved the people around the space. The building was motion, an organism. It was time in reinforced concrete. She looked up. It looked like a flower, the petals splayed in a distorted perspective, like a cubist painting, but following a mid-century logic. She was full, bursting, in love. That was how a new place took root inside. Searching for home, she was stretching herself, letting her love expand categories, to fit more in. Wright joining Niemeyer, peanut butter and jelly sandwiches joining acarajés. (Later, she would let in more of the landscape too: the rivers, Hudson, East, and others beyond the city; the beaches without palm trees; the deciduous trees, maples, blue cardinals, and button bushes; and later still, the prairie, and tundra, and the red of Arizona and New Mexico, joining the red of the dirt on her father's hands.)

When she got home from the Guggenheim that day, the Devil was waiting for her at her desk, backlit by the angled winter end-of-the-afternoon sun. The light painted his outline and the white walls golden, orange, peach. He asked how the writing was going. She said it was going okay. No, it was good, she corrected herself. She had just gotten some new things, something inside her to explore, but it wasn't in words yet. The Devil nodded; he understood what she meant, and he could feel that she was carrying it in her.

The Devil had something for her. He glanced at a potted plant that had died, sitting on the windowsill by her desk, dry fallen leaves surrounding three short skinny stalks. He opened his right hand. In the middle of it was a plant, a tiny succulent, just a bud, as if it had just sprouted from his palms. The bud opened into petallike but thick leaves, a little bud in the middle like the original inside them, which in turn opened its own leaves with its own little bud in the middle. The cycle continued, the plant growing, opening for her from its inner center, as if she were watching an accelerated stop-motion video of the process, but it was smooth, and live, and right in front of her. It stopped when there were about seven layers in a fractal pattern. It was a common succulent, found everywhere, Ikea, coffee shops, co-working spaces. But it was beautiful.

Sometimes, the Devil said, you had to let things germinate — sprout and grow. And later, you tended to them. The Devil looked at the writer's laptop open on the desk, the screen off in Sleep mode. Though, of course—he looked at the plant—he had sped things up a bit in this case. For effect. He smiled. The Devil angled his hand and let the plant slide into the pot by the window, where it replaced the dead one. Then he said its name: *Graptopetalum bellum*.

Petalum. Bellum. She had seen the plant so many times but never known its name. It sounded like a spell.

# TROPICÁLIA

*I'm only interested in what is not mine.*

—Oswald de Andrade, *The Cannibalist Manifesto*, 1928

*Fred, what we want is, I think, what everyone wants, and
what you and your viewers have—civilization . . . We want
to be civilized.*

—Brain Gremlin, *Gremlins II: The New Batch*, 1990

Sunday, August 20 🌘 Waning Crescent
(Day minus 1)

I woke from unsettling dreams to my mattress jingling with loose
change. I lay on my stiff back, armor-tight with tension. I raised my
head a little and saw my brown belly divided into sections, striped by
the sun slicing through half-open vertical blinds. The lines extended
and covered the room with bars. With a monstrous hangover, I peeled
off a penny stuck to the skin next to my belly button, then remembered my passport.

I stood up too quickly and shielded my right eye from a beam of
sunlight. Wincing at something hard digging into the sole of my foot,
I looked down and saw I stepped on my treasured *Gremlins* key chain,

fracturing my poor Gizmo's tiny plastic back. I was sweating. I closed the blinds. Part of my nightmare returned (sun, salt, me with an insect's legs, scurrying south on city streets).

My phone hid in my papers on global localization strategies (I worked with semiautomated corporate translation), betrayed only by its limp cord, hopelessly disconnected from a power source. Reflected on my dead screen, I looked like vermin. A dream, I reminded myself, and plugged in the phone. As I waited, I stood up and readjusted a crooked white framed triptych of a winking Pop Art Carmen Miranda, her three heads heavy with fruit. The screen turned on and I wiped away the notifications. No missed calls. No emails from work. My nausea gathered and condensed into a singularity in my stomach. That part had not been a dream. No messages about my missing passport. My passport, holding my H-1B work visa, was gone.

Sunday, August 13   ◖   Waning Gibbous

(Day minus 8)

I was having Cheerios for lunch on the shelf I IKEA-hacked into a counter in my kitchen, which was also my living room. I'd worked late on an analysis of our human translator testers the night before. It had gone well, and I was excited about what I might bring to my boss, Meredith, the following week. But I had overdone it and needed a break. So I spent most of my Sunday morning on Pinterest. My prewar studio impersonating a one-bedroom apartment was not as I wanted it yet, but getting there. The view was still water towers on this end and a dumpster on the other. But I had an exposed brick wall, tropical plants, including a monstera, a berimbau I couldn't play. Though I hadn't found anything on Pinterest that day (a bad sign).

I swiped out of the news Google had selected for me (rumors of raids in Queens, seven steps to boost your career, tips for watching the Great American Eclipse), then checked there were no emails from work. I needed to stop thinking about work (it had become even harder since Meredith mentioned a possible promotion). On the Brasileiros de Nova Iorque group, a post advertising a facial had three likes. Seven likes on a picture of a Minnie Mouse cake surrounded by brigadeiros. And 137 combined sad faces, angry faces, thumbs-up, at least one laughing emoji, and fifty comments on a post by a woman thinking about divorce but afraid for her green card application. The top comment began, "I get that there are many out there that don't respect the law. But if you choose to do things right (like I certainly do), there are only two ways: it's either a real marriage or an employer sponsors you. Now if you choose not to educate yourself, not to work hard, or . . ."

I stopped reading, startled by something moving on a spoon on the counter, just under where I was holding the phone. I thought it was a cockroach but realized the dark lump trapped at the center of the spoon had been my reflection. I heard a buzzing coming from the window. There was a fly there, trapped between the glass and the screen. I didn't want to kill it per se; I just wanted it gone. So I looked for help on YouTube, which led me to *The Fly*, a movie I hadn't seen since I was a child. I watched it instead of dealing with the real fly, and that was my Sunday. Nothing else happened, but the comments from the Brasileiros de Nova Iorque group stayed with me the whole day and through the night.

### Monday, August 14   🌗   Last Quarter
#### (Day minus 7)

That Monday, I missed my alarm and woke up late at eight thirty. I got ready in a panic. When Meredith had told me about a position opening up and briefly mentioned this one guy as my competitor, I'd imagined some guy in a skinny suit, with gelled hair and pointy, overly shiny brown leather shoes. I imagined him in the mirror, shaking his head at me as I hurried to brush my teeth. The position had to be mine. There were the usual things: yes, career, I needed more money. But mostly, I was entering the last year of my H-1B visa and needed to ask the company to sponsor my green card, as they had vaguely alluded to when I'd been hired.

I was about to leave but paused at the threshold of my open front door. I sent a message to Meredith, apologizing for running late. I told her there was trouble on the F line and that I would be there as soon as I could. Then I went back in and sat on my green velvet couch. I opened the Brasileiros de Nova Iorque group and scrolled through the posts on the president's tweets, the eclipse, and microblading. The woman wanting a divorce seemed to be gone. But I wasn't after her. I kept scrolling until I found the ICE thread. Those who had passports, visas, and green cards were arguing about whether to always carry them ("I thought that was just an Arizona thing," "How will they be able to tell," "In 25 years nobody has ever," "Well, they asked me," "If you have nothing to hide"). Of course, the rule didn't fully make sense, as a Brazilian guy who appeared white in his profile picture had pointed out in the group. If they stopped noncitizens to check their papers, wouldn't they have to stop citizens as well? How would they know whom to stop? It wasn't like noncitizens put stickers on their lapels indicating noncitizenship. He reminded me of the guy in the studio control room in *Gremlins 2*, mocking the logic of the "don't feed after midnight" rule, speculating what would happen to a gremlin crossing time zones. As he begins to laugh at his own jokes, a gremlin springs up and eats his face.

There it was, right after the comment on rumored ICE activity on the 7, the USCIS link. I clicked. The open-armed blue-and-white eagle greeted me in its familiar unnerving way. I read the passage ("every alien," "at all times," "personal possession," "alien registration," "comply," "guilty," "fined," "imprisoned," etc., etc.) again. Yes, supposedly, it applied to all of us. Anyone not considered a citizen had to be ready with the applicable papers. At all times.

I thought of my opponent for the promotion again. I imagined him thin, with a sharp jawline, blue eyes, black hair, walking into our building, taking confident sips of his morning kale smoothie. Fresh and ready for action, having started his day with yoga or spinning or both. I imagined Meredith's boss, Mr. Koning, and his lot of higher-ups nodding to one another in approval. They'd notice a commotion in the background, turn, and see me being shoved into a van while trying to appear professional in a pencil skirt. Handcuffed, I'd still wave meekly at Meredith, who would admit, embarrassed, that the woman being taken away by the authorities was the candidate she'd suggested for promotion.

I went back in for my passport, safely cocooned in a ziplock bag, inside a shoebox, under my bed. I opened the H-1B stamp page, hovered my fingers over my picture, the signature, the seal, just short of touching it. I closed the passport and put it inside a compartment in my respectable brown leather Banana Republic outlet bag and zipped it, then closed and buttoned the top flap.

On the train to work, I let go of the pole momentarily and searched for any new posts about H-1Bs on the Brasileiros de Nova Iorque group. I grabbed the pole again and clicked with my free hand on the link someone had posted of a forum that crowdsourced updates from applicants for various visas and calculated current processing times. But I lost reception before it opened. I had looked at the forum repeatedly and most likely wouldn't have found anything new, but I couldn't stop checking.

I swapped the hand holding the pole, brushed lightly against the hand of a blond woman, and apologized. She looked straight ahead. A message from Meredith popped up on my screen: "Everything is fine over here." Luckily, I was not meeting her first thing in the morning. And I still had a small buffer before the meeting with the translators. "I'm so sorry," I texted Meredith. I took a deep breath and went over the plan for the translators meeting again. I would walk to their back room, the same room where I'd worked when I first joined, then have them leave their cubicles and sit with me in a circle over cookies and coffee. Nothing formal. I would remind them again of how I had started just like them. How Marisa had helped me find everything on the first day of work, how Miki had stopped me from accidentally entering the men's bathroom. Then I would pivot to introducing the basics of the new rewards system. Not all the details on the points this time. I just hoped they understood the opportunity available to each of them. If only they could see it. I was lucky to have had Meredith help me. Maybe I could do the same for one of them. After the meeting, I'd go over the new targets with Meredith. I knew we could increase the output on our end if we just tightened the ship a bit. I was also thinking of a new metric, a simple addition requiring translators to rate the work of their colleagues as it moves through the workflow. It would be a chance for them to get more credit when they worked hard. And it would address our concern about individual accountability. Meredith would love it.

The train sped up. A white man in a suit reached for our pole, squeezing by a Latino man wearing jeans and work boots, who reminded me of somebody, though I couldn't tell whom. The blond woman sighed. I counted the five hands sharing the pole, including a woman—brown like me, but with electric-blue nail polish—who just managed to grab it with her fingertips. I couldn't see her face. Across the car, I spotted a muscular white man with a crew cut, dark gray pants, and a black polo shirt, sitting on one of the orange seats. A photograph from the Brasileiros de Nova Iorque group sprung to my memory: men in black shirts and sunglasses, "ICE" written on white letters on their backs. Without thinking, I ran my hand over the pocket carrying my passport. I wished I could get to work.

I realized the man reminded me of Jeff Goldblum, which was strangely reassuring. I thought of *The Fly*. Brundle's tragic and hilariously gross journey from scientist to giant fly. His skin smooth, then stubble, then blisters, then gooey raw meat. All done in analog in 1986. The whole thing had to do with movement, teletransportation, which fascinated me. He entered a pod a normal guy. He couldn't see it, but by the time he stepped out of the other pod, he'd already become a monster.

As the doors finally slid open at my stop, another message from Meredith arrived: "Don't worry about a thing."

Sunday, August 20 ● Waning Crescent
(Day minus 1)

The passport lasted less than a week being carried everywhere in my bag. There were a couple of times when it felt right to have it there, close to me. That one time in the subway; that afternoon walking under the rows of American flags, by the rows of police (or military or both) at Penn Station; that time going through the security desk and turnstile when I joined Meredith for a client meeting in a different building. But mostly, there was the fear I would lose it. It was like being resigned to having a fly trapped in a room: Sometimes you forgot it was there, and then it came back buzzing, and you had to wait until it stopped and you forgot it again.

And now here I was. Two caplets of Tylenol, a mug of water, and my phone lay on my imitation-marble coffee table. I called the Mandarin Hotel bar. I balanced my phone between my head and my shoulder as I waited, squeezing the sides of my broken Gizmo key chain as if trying to undo the split along its back. With the back open, its head no longer stayed firmly in place. Nobody answered at the bar. I tried the main hotel, where the receptionist informed me the bar opened at four. I thought of the USCIS passage ("alien," "at all times," "personal," "possession," "guilty"), sitting among the other words on their site all this time. And the same text in dusty books before there was such a thing as a USCIS website, the letters set in bookshelves while I played in our muddy backyard in Brazil, my cousins laughing as I imitated ALF's dubbed Portuguese voice. And the same words on other shelves somewhere in the US before that, long before I'd been born.

I put up my broken Gizmo up on my bookshelf, next to a sad baby banana seedling I'd ordered online, its two little leaves wilted and browned. The shelves were full of classics I hadn't read. A few titles in Portuguese (*Memórias Póstumas de Brás Cubas, A Paixão Segundo G.H., O Estrangeiro*), the rest in English. Part of an effort to convey that I am a particular kind of person I couldn't have pretended to be back in Brazil. An ambition that is only possible because Americans don't know what my accent in Portuguese, or my name, or my parents' names convey about our place in the world.

Gizmo's head fell off and rolled close to the edge of the shelf, but I caught it right before it dropped and carefully placed it next to its cracked headless body. At the vintage store where I'd found it my first year in the US, there had been a couple in mismatched plaid shirts ahead of me in line who saw the key chain first. They looked at it with mild interest and put it back. When the woman said the word "gremlins," it took a second for my brain to map the word as she pronounced it to the way the word had lived in my head as a child. We said "gremilins" in Portuguese, that extra *i* added like a drop of water to the back of a mogwai, giving rise to an additional syllable. When I realized the key chain was Gizmo, I reached for it immediately. I estimated how many times I'd watched *Gremlins 2* in Sessão da Tarde reruns in Brazil. Every afternoon I ate lunch with my brother and sister and watched the soap operas. After the novelas came the few movies TV Globo had dubbed in Portuguese. The same recognizable voices regurgitated out of the mouths of different actors, over and over in all the movies they showed. How strange to feel at that moment that the little Gizmo was more rightly mine than theirs, that American couple who'd clearly missed the movie's brilliance.

I pushed the broken pieces back, farther into the shelf, to make sure they didn't fall, and went to get ready to leave.

Saturday, August 19 ● Waning Crescent
(Day minus 2)

I last checked on my passport late Saturday afternoon, just before I walked out with Meredith. She had found a way to bring me along for drinks with Mr. Koning, her boss. As I'd been about to leave work the previous day, she had held my shoulders, looked me in the eye, and told me the timing was perfect. I had been giddy about it all afternoon, but now I was worried about what I was supposed to do, about not messing up my great chance. We were at an exclusive spot at the Mandarin Hotel. A place just like I'd imagined people like them went: a little *Mad Men*, somewhere along a lineage of leather Chesterfields, dark wood, and shelves filled with matching book covers, seamlessly mixed with dark mid-century furniture. And those floor-to-ceiling windows again. Here the city appeared brighter and closer. It felt as if the people in the other buildings could see everything and everyone, including me. It felt familiar, though I had never been there. A déjà vu. I couldn't place it, and that made me more nervous. I ordered a Malbec.

I sipped it quietly as they discussed projects outside my department. Meredith alternated her posture: sometimes sitting back and propping her elbows on the back of the chair, grabbing her whiskey on the rocks in the relaxed "I don't care" manner of Mr. Koning and other seemingly powerful men in the restaurant; sometimes sitting up, cross-legged, her arms close to her body as if trying not to occupy space; sometimes leaning into the table and touching her hair, almost flirtatiously. Mr. Koning didn't notice how she advanced and retreated strategically, slowly gaining space. She indulged all his interruptions and came back around in a gentle way, until her points were made. Even after everything Meredith had taught me and what I'd learned by watching her, there was so much more. I was struggling to find an opening. I realized I was hiding behind my wineglass, not varying my posture, not saying anything. Mr. Koning didn't seem to notice me. I put my glass down and leaned into the table slightly, bending toward him. I decided my focus now would be to appear fascinated by whatever he said (which was?). I knew Meredith would manage to bring me into the conversation in a manner that was most advantageous to me. I waited for her cue. She always looked out for me.

Maybe the strange familiarity I felt were the large windows, reminding me of the view in the office. Those nights when I'd snuck out of my cubicle to work alone by a window in the conference room, after everyone had gone home. Yes, this was familiar. But there was something else too.

When I was close to finishing my glass, she asked what I was drinking. Mr. Koning wasn't looking, fiddling with his phone, so she shook her head and scrunched her face at her whiskey. We both smiled. Before I could answer, she said softly that I had to try her favorite drink, a passion fruit Caipijito. I always felt stupidly possessive of caipirinhas, which I didn't usually drink. Already my brain was activating the heuristic script for expressing how the drink conformed or deviated from the elusive original and an explanation of how caipirinhas really were back at home (as if they were really that different). But I knew I shouldn't deny her. Besides, it sounded like a good drink.

Mr. Koning answered his phone.

"Fantastic!" He nodded to both of us, still talking to his caller (the second time he had looked at me, the first being a glance during introductions). He stood and headed out toward the elevators.

Meredith audibly exhaled. Her body seemed to soften as she fluffed up her blond hair with both hands. She explained that she didn't always get to come out with Aldert (Mr. Koning) and that we were only here for his pre-drinks, while he waited for whatever important people he was here to see. But it didn't matter, she continued. It was still a good opportunity. She was excited she finally got to bring me this time.

"It's good for you to be on his radar," Meredith mock whispered, touching my hand with the corner of hers and looking about the room conspiratorially. "Sometimes it's productive, but sometimes he's just in the mood to be entertained. Then we just have to be agreeable and split without being awkward, before the big guys come."

"Got it." I nodded. The drink was delicious. I was so grateful to her. This place was perfect. I held both her hands in a way I had never done before. "Thank you, Meredith."

Meredith smiled. She'd been happy with me the whole day. I wasn't sure why. "How's the cocktail?"

"So good." I took another sip.

"Oh my God, isn't it though?" She looked even more pleased. "You are doing great. I knew you would."

Meredith had been a little guarded when I first met her. But with time, she saw that I both worked hard and didn't cause trouble. I was able to understand things she could not talk about to anyone else at work, often to do with navigating power structures as a woman. I wouldn't start petitions or go running to HR if she talked about things as they truly were. One day, she sternly called me into her office at the end of a quarterly status meeting, but her summons had only been an excuse to remove me from a conversation with a guy from another department, known to be creepy. She gradually opened up and became a mentor as well as my boss. Sometimes, like right then, I wanted to hug her, which would've been silly, so I smiled at her instead. She smiled back. I hoped she knew how grateful I was.

I looked at the moon through the windows of the Mandarin Hotel. A thinning curve, most of it disappearing into darkness, pulsating faintly, almost a mirage. I realized what this place, the large dark glass windows reminded me of: *Gremlins 2*. I had framed an eight by ten version of the film poster and hung it on the wall between my bedroom and bathroom. The illustration showed a solid wooden desk and the scratched back of a plush leather chair. Only the hand of the creature facing the view of the city at night was visible, its skin scaly and green, its black-clawed finger lingering in the air, about to tap down the ashes from a lit cigar. They hadn't dubbed the gremlins when they sang "New York, New York." The creatures performed and ran amok to the sound of Sinatra as the terrified humans did whatever they could to keep them from coming out of their dark glass enclosure—and now here I was. New York City outside those large windows. Meredith and I clinked our glasses with the last sips of our Caipijitos. She ordered two more.

I wondered what time it was ("always midnight somewhere") as I stabbed an olive. I thought of the green skin on the hand dangling the cigar. I thought of how the green in steaming hatching gremlin cocoons looked like the neon-green light coming out of the pod in the promo poster of *The Fly*. I thought of myself sitting there, my body filled with American proteins. American water. American sugar. The alcohol taking over my brain and liver. I remembered reading that it took ten years for a human skeleton to be completely replaced through cell renewal. I had American bones now. I'd thought I was the eater, but America had been eating me the whole time, from within.

Sunday, August 20  Waning Crescent
(Day minus 1)

My gaze crawled down the six flights of my walk-up, from the middle of each step to the shadows in the corners, searching for my passport.

Outside, the sun was inhuman and oppressive. I pulled the brim of my hat closer to my large dark sunglasses. Across the street, a man walked a pug. A couple with matching cups of coffee passed by me, followed by a woman talking on her cell phone.

"Home," she said, and laughed. I searched the bases of trees, flower beds littered with cigarette butts, trash cans, the ground near the garbage bags piled high on the sidewalks, trying to undo my steps from last night.

I stopped by the tree where I'd been sick the night before, wincing at what I might see. But there seemed to be no trace of me. I reversed the route I'd walked, looking down between the streetlamps, now under bright sunlight. I retraced the course to the subway station twice and found nothing. A man dressed in black crossed the street in my direction, startling me. He kept walking. I crossed my arms. My head throbbed; the city pulsated with heat, pressing down on me. I descended into the subway station.

It was only 2:55 P.M. when I reached the Mandarin Hotel. I had one hour to kill, but I was too nervous to wait in the hotel lobby. Those impossibly high ceilings, granite, and glass. It was clear I didn't belong there. So I left and wandered the blocks between the hotel and the subway again, eyeing the overflowing trash cans. I sat on the bench across the hotel, then looked at the USCIS website for the list of requirements for an InfoPass appointment.

Saturday, August 19 ● Waning Crescent
(Day minus 2)

Meredith and I cheered at the arrival of our second round of cocktails.

"I knew when I saw you that you were different from the other people you worked with," she said.

I laughed and thanked her. The Mandarin Hotel swayed a little.

"I don't mean anything by it. Nothing to do with, you know . . ."

I didn't know, but I was smiling.

"They just seemed like such slackers! And you, you worked your ass off to get that first promotion."

It felt good to hear. I did work a lot. And I paid attention. But something about what she was saying bothered me. It was difficult to understand it on the spot. I ran my hands over my face, then placed them on the table, trying to ground myself. Meredith had hardly spent any time with them. I remembered myself talking, telling the translators about Miki and Marisa on my first day again. I had rehearsed my speech so many times in my head, it was hard to separate the anecdote as I told it from my memory of actually meeting them. But Meredith had been so generous to me. This feeling too, whatever it was, would fade. It was fading already. I took a sip of water.

"Thank you, Meredith."

"Oh, don't thank me! Thank you!" She raised her glass, took a gulp, and proceeded to tell me how my idea to rebrand translation as a Bidirectional Quality Assurance option had been great, but that the International Reputation Monitoring package had been a genius move. "I mean, before, it was all that talk about cultural competency, blah, blah, blah. It'd never worked. Until you pitched it like that. You're gonna be a rock star."

I didn't have to try to smile at that. I'd been too hard on her. My work never went unnoticed with Meredith. And it wasn't just empty words. She always tried to give me credit in front of others and to get what she could for me as a reward. A day off when things were not too busy, a strategic introduction, a recommendation that I be the one to take on new responsibilities. I took another sip of my Caipijito, delicious and sweet, a wonderful invention. I was glad I'd come up with BQA and IRM too. They were how I paid my rent and bought my green velvet couch.

Meredith fished a basil leaf out of her drink with some difficulty and bit it, then continued about how brilliant I'd been to reposition the translation piece not as a boring administrative necessity but as a value-adding expansion of our client's brand. "What I'm trying to say is"—she stirred her drink—"you got it. You're gonna be promoted."

I hugged her. And I felt so happy as I thanked her. Or did I? I did. I felt happy. Relieved. But it was different from what I'd imagined. A little more subdued. As if I'd already celebrated and now needed to work on the next thing. She was talking about how the promotion was part of the "whole department revamp thing" and something about

Mr. Koning and the board. I was drunk but put effort into making sure my face revealed only pure joy.

Mr. Koning was walking back to the table, adjusting the lapel of his suit over his slightly stumpy body, running his hand over his thick but graying hair. He seemed surprised to see us at the table, as if he'd forgotten we were there.

"This one is getting promoted!" Meredith pointed at me.

"Oh, that's nice." He looked at both of us briefly, then at the screen of his phone as he placed it on the table.

"She was instrumental in the BQA and IRM packages."

"The what?" He looked at Meredith without much interest.

"The new services JBS picked up."

"Oh, JBS!" He perked up. "JBS was good!" He looked at me as if seeing my face for the first time. "Nice work!" He offered me his hand for a handshake. A single shake, brief but forceful, like a salute. Then he looked away toward the bar. He spotted a waiter and motioned for him to come to the table. "That's great, ladies. I'm glad we got to celebrate." He looked at his phone. "Now, I'm afraid my time's up."

It took me a second to remember what Meredith had said earlier. He meant we had to leave.

Meredith and I both stumbled into the elevator.

"This'll be so good for you. We'll lipo some fat off that department, make it more efficient. Make ourselves some money." She pressed the number forty-five, which was where we already were. "Whoops!" She pressed L and leaned on the brushed metal wall beside the vintage-style buttons that lit up and faded as we passed the floors. "I don't know if I should tell you this, but . . ."

I leaned on the wall on my side too.

"Oh, what the hell. You're cool, and you may as well learn these things. It always helps to know how things work." She closed her eyes and said, "They specifically wanted someone to, you know . . . We're beginning to look bad at certain meetings, depending on who the client is. Don't get me wrong. They wanted someone good." She brushed a strand of hair away from her eyes, even though they were closed. "They wanted some diversity, but someone who wouldn't, you know, stand out too much." She paused and opened her eyes briefly, as if checking the effect of what she'd just said.

I began to feel angry. Not at Meredith. No. It was at myself, my face. My face had told her it was OK to continue.

"There was only you and that other guy I mentioned. Some Eduardo from another department. Do you know him?"

"Eduardo?" Maybe I'd heard the name or maybe not. I tried to search for a memory. Nothing. I tried to name the kale smoothie-drinking man I'd imagined "Eduardo."

"Oh, are you guys, like, friends or something?"

"No, no. I don't know any Eduardos."

"Oh, good." She touched my hand. She'd slid down the wall a little and adjusted her position back up. "Anyway, I just found out this afternoon that they picked you! I was so happy. I mean, you're amazing, in my team. And also"—Meredith raised a fist and let it go limp—"we need more women!"

The elevator arrived; Meredith steadied herself from the jolt, straightened up, and walked out. I followed her through the foyer and out of the hotel. There was a warm breeze. I felt temporarily sober with the sound of passing traffic.

"Don't tell anyone," she said.

"Of course."

She looked up at me as she entered her Uber. "The other guy, Eduardo—he turned out"—she looked into her purse, having accidentally dropped her phone there—"to be DACA, and you know"—she found her phone and smiled at me—"who knows what's happening with all that." She closed the door and said through the open window, "You lucky girl. Congratulations!"

Sunday, August 20  ● Waning Crescent

(Day minus 1)

I returned close to 4 P.M. A man came and wiped the bar counter. Another picked up the chairs and stools that were upside down on the tables and whistled, half sang, and hummed to accompany the song playing softly in the back of the bar. I recognized it, the one with Anitta and Poo Bear. I walked over.

I asked if they had a lost and found. The man shrugged.

I tried Spanish. "He perdido algo."

"Brasileira?" he asked in perfect Portuguese.

I nodded, sensing my voice would falter.

He told me to wait and went to get the bartender inside.

The other worker looked at me with concern. "Estás bien?"

I asked him for a glass of water, and he got me one straightaway. The other man returned and gestured me to the VIP room.

The room, which I hadn't known existed the night before, sat above the main room. Through its windows, I could see the table where we had sat and all the other tables downstairs, and the city. Though here, in daytime and from this angle, it felt as if I could see the city but it couldn't see me.

A blond woman I didn't recognize from the previous night was polishing glasses by the cash register. She showed me a pair of sunglasses and a credit card.

I shook my head. "Are you sure there's not anything else?"

"It doesn't seem like it. What did you lose?"

"My ID." I felt ashamed. "I mean, my passport."

She frowned a little, then nodded, opened the cash register, and lifted the fasteners over the cash. She bent to look deep into the drawer, then under the counter, then asked me to wait and went to the back. Reflected on the corner of the mirror behind the bar and mirrored back wall, I saw myself doubled, tripled, quadrupled. The woman came back frowning, but when she saw me, her eyebrows reversed like a rising bridge. She sucked her lips inward and shook her head.

Monday, August 21  ●  Syzygy/New Moon
(Day 0: Occultation)

I bring all the documents I have to work, planning to duck out to a USCIS office and try for an InfoPass appointment. The social media scoop on the Brasileiros de Nova Iorque group was that it took about six months from an official appointment. At least, that's how it'd been before the election. Or for green card holders. Worst-case scenario, I might need to go back to Brazil to get a new H-1B stamp (that would be the worst; I can't take a vacation now). Or I might be able to legally stay put without a stamp as long as I didn't leave the country. It wasn't clear, but either way, I will make things work. What else can happen? Nothing else will happen. As terrible as it is, Deus me perdoe, they are only going for undocumented people and maybe people with DACA, I tell myself.

I don't know what kind of paperwork HR may require with the promotion. I arrive early to prepare myself for a productive day at work to show everyone they made the right decision. The promotion hasn't happened officially yet, but it will be formally announced sometime soon, Meredith assured me. I want to be finished with the unpleasant tasks by lunch and then go to USCIS. Dragging it out longer will not help matters. Ultimately, the truth is I have no choice over what will happen. If I don't do what I am about to do, someone else will. The only difference is that I would likely be fired too. I feel confident in my choices, I reassure myself. Lucien is frequently late, smokes too much, and is too often behind in both his deadlines and word-per-hour quotas. Plus, I fear his whole work-life balance attitude may be contagious. Miki is an excellent translator. But, as much as I feel terrible for her, the demand is low for her region, and we can get by with freelancers. I'll write her a good letter of recommendation. Then there is Marisa. A good writer, deep in her deliberations. But she just doesn't seem to get that our clients are a corporate American audience. What they want is added value to their brands, not the cultural nuance she spends hours trying to subtly imply in her work. I don't have much room to choose people given how many I am required to let go. My list makes sense. There is no way for me to know everyone's situation and immigration status. Even if I could dig that up, justifying my choices in those terms would only weigh against the very people I try to protect. And it would drag me along with them.

I leave the building at 2:15 P.M., planning to come back and stay late to make up for leaving early. By the time I walk out through the revolving doors, it is already easier to push away the image of Marisa sitting across the desk from me, her petite shoulders hunched as she stares blankly out the window. The sight of her reminded me of that day the fly was buzzing while trapped in between the glass and the screen of my window. I feel bad for her, I remind myself. As stressful as the situation is, it's been good, in a way. The whole thing with the passport occupied my thoughts, distracting me from this. Sometimes things have a way of working out.

I squint at the light bouncing off the glass windows of Crate &
Barrel. I can hardly see the outlines of the sofas and lamps, and the
glass reflects the silhouettes of people rushing to and from their lunch
breaks. Instead of wondering, as I do from time to time, if any of them
will be fired, I wonder if any of them have done the firing. I feel sorry
for all of them. And for myself, and for Marisa. And Eduardo. But my
sympathy is of no use to anyone. I spot my reflection, adjust a strand
of hair that was out of place, and keep walking.

A block from the USCIS office, the sky gets a little darker, as if from
a very dark cloud. But the sky is clear. The city is made strange by the
light, the shadows slightly distorted. In the distance, people stand as
if frozen, staring at the ground. Others look up wearing cardboard
glasses. Of course. I have forgotten. The eclipse.

I remember to look down to not damage my vision. The light is
painting curves on the sidewalk. I splay my fingers, place my hands on
top of each other to make a grid, and watch my shadow's transforma-
tion (I picture the shadow of a human turning into a werewolf in an
old silent movie). Something moves on the ground, blurry under the
edge of my telephone screen. I shift my focus and see the cockroach
run in between one pile of trash bags, hiding under the dark plastic. I
feel a tenderness for it. Everyone wants to squash it dead, and yet here
it is keeping me company. I wonder if it notices anything about the
strangeness of the celestial bodies moving above it. I shift my gaze to
a crack on the sidewalk and see the dappled light bent into the shape
of the moon, asserting herself in the sky. I imagine she can see me,
looking down at her, surrounded by a sea of crescents, a thousand Cs.

{  }

There was something wrong with the air-conditioning at the DMV; the writer was sweating on one of the red plastic chairs, holding her number. "W663" blinked on the screen. She wished she had brought her notebook. Or something more immediately distracting than the volume on Saint Augustine she'd borrowed from the library. The chairs were too close. The man next to her spread his legs beyond the edges of his seat. She had to squeeze hers together so they wouldn't touch. He wore a black shirt with a small American flag, a white eagle printed on his sleeve, and gray camo shorts; his skinny legs were a pasty pink with long black hairs that were close to touching her. The writer googled "do objects ever really touch? Atoms." The number on the DMV screen didn't move. The air was thick, damp, and smelled slightly of sweat. She scanned the website linked to the first result. No, things never really touch, in the physical sense. Touch is how your brain interprets what is really a form of repulsion. Particles and waves, duality, etc. Something like that. It was hard to concentrate. The man chuckled at something on his phone; his torso moved up and down. At least they weren't touching.

The number on the DMV screen changed. It wasn't her

number. The man looked up and looked back at his phone. It wasn't his number either, but it didn't seem to bother him too much. At least he was calm. He was still smiling at his phone. The reason the writer didn't like the man probably had less to do with his leg hair so close to her than with the fact she was afraid of him. His black-and-white American flag, the angry eagle. When she'd first arrived in the US, many years ago, she had a brief period when she was unaware of the complicated web of icons all around her. But she learned, slowly, without even noticing. And as her awareness had changed, so had the symbols, always adapting slightly to the currents and the fashion. Now they were hypervisible to her: The tiny flags, the big flags in color, the black-and-white flags, the single red lines and single blue lines. And more recently, the election signs, the red hats. A few weeks before, they'd visited Peter's relatives out of town, and she found herself parking a little farther down the street to avoid stopping in front of a house with two large American flags at the front. Peter's aunt commented on how she could park closer. The writer had smiled and said she had gotten confused by the GPS. And now here she was next to this man, both of them maybe united by their need to get a Real ID, after the Real ID Act was passed as part of a defense bill years ago.

"L413. L413," shouted a curly-haired lady with reading glasses behind the counter. On the screen "L413" blinked frantically. The lady shrugged. The screen read "L414." The man groaned at the change and slapped his right leg. Not his number, again. The writer crossed her legs tighter, tugged down the bottom of her shirt slightly, and smoothed the bottom of her skirt over her calves. She wondered how the man read his own T-shirt, if he understood it in the same way she did, or if the story he told himself was couched in other words, tangled in all sorts of other things. She wondered if a desire to instill fear was overt, on the surface in his mind, or if he could consciously detect any of it. Or maybe it was all in her head. Maybe he just liked how the flag, and the eagle, and the camo shorts looked. How could she tell anything? Five minutes ago, she'd believed the fiction created by her brain that things touched. She squeezed the hard round lip of the chair, the edge away from the man. She got her book out of her bag to distract her.

The man faced his phone down and yawned. He looked around him, glancing briefly at her. He closed his leg slightly but was still beyond the boundaries of his seat. She did her best to keep a neutral expression: not friendly or encouraging of conversation, but not confrontational. She wished the man were gone. The man was about to say something to her. But he paused, put his hand on his stomach, and frowned. He got up abruptly, ran to the security guy at the front, and asked him where the bathroom was. The writer relaxed her legs and let them take up the space of her seat. Two rows ahead, the Devil walked in, wearing a suit and a Panama hat. He grabbed a number, then winked at her, tilting his hat.

She looked toward the bathroom where the man had run with a worried expression. The Devil shrugged. Then wiggled his fingers no and pointed at himself, saying it hadn't been him.

The writer narrowed her eyes at him but smiled. The Devil sat down where the man had been. The AC was suddenly working again, and the Devil's warmth was pleasant. The air smelled faintly of someone freshly showered, a little like Peter, a subtle soapy sweetness. The Devil's legs were nicely contained within the boundaries of his own seat. She wanted to hug him but couldn't. She said he looked good. He was dressed very formally, a light purple, almost white, handkerchief was folded perfectly in his breast pocket. He wore cuff links. He said something about time zones, a ball to get back to, after he checked in on her.

*Thank you*, she thought. *But is the guy from before* OK?

The Devil told her the man was quite happy and relieved at the moment. The Devil mentioned he had met the same man before, in that same DMV. They had chatted and shared MoonPies from the vending machine. The Devil loved the DMV. So many stories. Besides, the man was not that bad in the grand scheme of things. "The grand scheme of things." One time, she and the Devil had been in an Airbnb, hanging in a Jacuzzi he had made magically clean and extra bubbly. The Devil had said he hated "the grand scheme of things," but that was what he had to work with. "The grand scheme of things" was in no way his fault. How could it be, really? Now at the DMV, he looked at her book sitting on her lap and raised his eyebrow with a suspicious expression. He asked if she had to be into that stuff, might he suggest Nyssa or, more recently, Kotsko, the romantics, or so many others instead of that guy—he pointed to Saint Augustine on the cover with a bitter expression. She picked up her phone to write the names down, but he stopped and waved a hand, dismissing her, when she asked him to repeat it. He asked her not to worry about it; it wasn't his place; it was silly, really. When she saw he wasn't going to get into it, she turned her screen to him instead, showing the article on atoms touching. He smiled and scooted closer to her, and she did the same toward him. Their legs almost touched. She lifted her hand off her lap and brought it close to his. He hovered his just above hers, as if they were frozen in the moment just before they held hands. They stayed like that for a couple of seconds. Then a small notebook appeared on his hand, and he passed it to her. A pen bookmarked the next blank page. She took it and smiled at him, and her number was called. She got up.

As she walked to the booth, she saw the man walking back from the bathroom. He looked well, content, the color back in his face.

She held her notebook in her left hand as she looked at the camera. The DMV lady asked the writer to remove her glasses, and she did. The flash went off. When she put the glasses back on, the writer saw the man again, through the afterimage of the flash. He was aiming to go back to his old seat. But he paused, looking at an older woman who was also moving toward it. She was white, with gray hair in a ponytail, and had a slight limp. The man stopped, discretely letting her take the seat. The writer looked for the Devil. But the Devil was gone.

# ANTROPÓFAGA

She devoured tiny Americans that slid out of a vending machine. Their thin metallic plastic packages almost opened themselves when punctured. Emerging with their tiny hands on either side of the rip, they declared their nutritional value (calcium, sugar, fat, 350 milligrams of synthetic protein). So many times she decided to diet and promised no more Americans. But she always walked by with an eye on the spot between the Ruffles and the Doritos, salivating. And before she could think there she was again, inserting the coins, hot and sweaty from her palms, into the machine's mouth.

The first had been a pinkish overweight man—flowery shirt, white sneakers, and socks biting at his thick ankles. He laughed and talked to invisible friends, pointing at things only he could see. He didn't notice when she lifted him, her index finger and thumb under his damp little armpits. Holding a selfie stick with a phone the size of a lentil, he posed in front of her giant open mouth, as if she were the Statue of Liberty. Right after the timer triggered the picture, Béia had swallowed him whole.

The machine had always been there. But she had never given it much thought before that first time, the first Monday of the year, a

January polar-vortex morning, so cold that it felt cruel. She hadn't slept well after a phone fight with her ex-boyfriend. Her kitchen sink was full of her new roommate's dirty dishes topped by a lipstick-rimmed wineglass. Béia was not able to gather the appetite for breakfast or the energy to figure out a packed lunch. When she got to the hospital and began work, the back-and-forth of her mop over the speckled light-green floor carried her like a current to the corridor, the familiar yelling of Fox News gradually fading as she moved away from the waiting room. And there, she found herself alone with the machine, its chocolate, chips, and Coca-Cola shining bright under the strategic white light.

Propping her hand and chin on the mop handle and facing the machine, she grew angry. She thought of the long hours in the hospital with that stringy, wet head, disgusting even when soaked in pungent disinfectant. The lazy roommate who'd replaced her boyfriend. The money she never managed to save. The many times she'd stayed quiet or smiled or thanked people without wanting to. The child, dog, house without a fence, and wedding that went down the drain in a counterclockwise swirl before ever happening. Grinding her molars, she hunted for coins in the pockets of her ugly uniform. And even though she was hungry, she was driven as much by rebellion as hunger. She wanted to do something she was not supposed to do.

She hadn't planned to come back the very next day. Before things had turned in her life, she had always brought fruit, rice, and beans, which she cooked simply but with care, pre-frying the grains in garlic and onions, a couple of bay leaves infusing a subtle fragrance to the beans. But in the past few months, it had been so difficult to do anything. And that day, a few minutes before lunch, she was putting away her basket with the cleaning cloth and spray when a hand tapped her three times on the shoulder. The pale woman sucked a bright pink liquid from her see-through plastic cup and see-through straw. Without interrupting her suction, she indicated with the bottom of her cup and a raise of her eyebrows a broken version of her beverage spread out on the floor. Ice cubes slid on a pallid-pink puddle between the dome lid and the body of the cup, opened wide like the mouth of the woman's child, who now screamed for his lost drink from beside her.

It was almost lunchtime, but Béia couldn't leave the mess there. Somebody would sue, or she'd get fired, both things easy to happen in the US. The woman interpreted Béia's hesitation as a lack of understanding. Her lips let go of the straw, and she tried to explain: "Limpiar? Por favor? Gracias!"

Béia nodded, gave the woman a deflated smile, and went after the orange cone, the bucket, the mop.

Béia had a meeting at two where they evaluated goals and objectives against performance for everyone in her wing. As she waited in the long cafeteria line, she could not stop thinking of the three taps on her shoulder and the screaming child. She had a secret thought, which embarrassed but consoled her a little: the truth was, Béia didn't even like children. But the consolation was diminished by the correction that followed: Béia only knew she didn't like other people's children.

Hungry and impatient, she stepped out of the line and returned to the machine. Out of the package came a cowboy with muddy jeans, boots, and a hat. He licked his index finger and lifted it to feel the direction of the wind. When she picked him up, he was shielding his eyes from the imaginary sun, his hands resembling a salute over his eyebrows. Facing her mouth, he concentrated on the horizon as if searching for an approaching tornado.

She knew eating from a vending machine was unhealthy. But she had so little now. Even if the satisfaction she got was brief and superficial, it was something, something she could give herself. So she went back. Three more times that week. And four the following two weeks, after she'd made a pact with herself to alternate days. Sometimes during lunchtime, sometimes at the end of her shift, and on the worst days, earlier, in the midmorning. She swallowed an aging Southern belle — blond, skinny, and lipsticked — in tasteful clothes. Then a woman whose hair needed washing, wearing Minnie Mouse ears and carrying a Dora the Explorer backpack. Then a bearded hipster holding a bottle of craft beer. He seemed to be in the middle of giving a disinterested but intelligent opinion, the punch line indicated by an unenthusiastic raise of his eyebrows, just before she swallowed him. It became a difficult habit to stop, an annoying and persistent urge, like a mosquito bite that kept itching, even after the skin had been scratched raw.

Wednesdays were off days, when Béia was supposed to stay away from the machine. So that early February morning, Béia snuck a cup from the coffee maker in the back filing room to distract herself from her cravings. Rosa was there, checking the cleaning logs.

Béia took a sip of the coffee, weak but sweet, at least, before she finally spoke. "Rosa?"

"Sí, B." Rosa kept her eyes on the filing cabinet, moving her right index finger over the files. But she touched Béia's shoulder lightly with her left hand.

"Do you ever" — Béia swallowed — "you know, eat from that vending machine?"

"Machine?" Rosa found a folder and pulled it out of the cabinet. She opened it and frowned. Then she looked at Béia and smiled. "What machine, B?"

"You know, the one in that corridor, off the waiting room."

"Ah. I don't know." Rosa laid her folder at the top of the cabinet, let her hand rest there as she looked up, trying to remember. "Maybe. I can't remember, but I don't think so. Isn't it a bunch of tasteless porquerias? I heard those things jam and eat your money." Rosa looked down and picked up her folder. Then her gaze moved up again, toward the PA system. It was calling her name. "Have to go, guapinha." She turned but paused at the door on her way out as if realizing something. She smiled at Béia. "Mira, if you like that stuff, who cares about what anyone thinks? And what's the point of worrying about ingredients, is it organic, does it come from this place or that other place, yadda, yadda, yadda? You are going to eat it anyway, right? Might as well enjoy it and not torture yourself. Things are hard enough, mi'ja." Rosa blew Béia a kiss and turned toward the door again. "Buen provecho, guapa," she said, walking away.

That week Béia swallowed a bodybuilder in an American-flag Speedo, posing before her as if she were a mirror. Then a frat boy drinking from a red plastic cup, while nodding his head slightly to a beat, as if a mob of college kids were yelling at him, "Drink! Drink! Drink!" Then a policeman who held up his gun and pulled the trigger right as he fell into her mouth.

On Friday, Béia approached Patricia in the locker room after they were done with their shifts. Patricia had just finished filling out her brows with a dark pencil as Béia asked what she thought about the machine, if she had ever used it.

Patricia stopped applying a layer of gloss to her bottom lip and turned to Béia, holding the brush in midair. "Ai, Béia, who cares about some stupid machine? Put your feet on the ground, amiga." Patricia shook her head. "This is what happens when you spend all your time in this place." She turned back to the mirror. "Let's get out of here."

She finished applying gloss and pressed her lips together, then opened them a few times to spread it, like a beautiful little fish, the kind you might find in the waiting room at pediatrics. Patricia sighed and looked at Béia sympathetically. "You need to have more fun in life. Go out sometimes. Come to the pagode with me tonight. It's so much fun." She held one of Béia's hands. "It'll do you good."

Béia was not ready to go out yet. But she'd begun, slowly, to get used to everything that had happened during the past few months. She smiled again, once in a while. And she wasn't dreading going home. Earlier that week, the roommate had begun watching Netflix in the living room and asked Béia to join her. The two laughed and talked about the show, a series set in the 1960s in America that everyone had watched ten years before, and Béia realized how she'd missed having some company when she got back home at night. After that, the dishes the roommate left didn't annoy her as much in the morning. She found it somewhat endearing now, a reminder of her company the previous night.

The rest of February, she ate a woman with a pink pussy hat; a bus driver; a biker, bearded and tattooed; and an older man in a light-green polo shirt, with a barely there comb-over, dunking what appeared to be tiny biscotti into a porcelain teacup. Then a woman holding a plate and serving herself from an invisible buffet. Then a curly-haired brown woman consulting what seemed to be a book, then typing on her laptop.

Béia managed to spend the first week of March away from the machine, a small accomplishment that reassured her that she could stop anytime. If she wanted to. The following Monday, she was finally feeling good and well rested. Humming an Anitta song in the laundry room, she grabbed a pile of warm cleaning cloths from the dryer, then went to one of the windowed patient rooms, where she sprayed the cleaning product and started wiping the windowsill. Someone had brought a mixed spring bouquet for the patient who slept under the soft sunlight. She was a thin woman, probably in her twenties, who looked healthier than when she'd arrived a few weeks before, despite the clear plastic cannula still attached to her nose. Béia rearranged the bunch a little, spacing some of the flowers. She took out a limp, dying lilac and threw it in the trash. The bouquet looked fresh again, and the room was clean, pleasant even. She left in good spirits. The hospital was not very busy that day, the corridors calm. She decided to take five minutes to sit outside in the small patch of garden on that sunny day, even if it was still cold. The machine was on the way. She thought about what Rosa and Patricia had said. Maybe she should enjoy herself a little more. This was her life now. She bent over and grabbed a packet from the chute of the machine and went outside.

She inhaled the cold air, closed her eyes for a minute, feeling the sun's dimmed warmth on her cheeks, dark orange behind her eyelids. She ripped the bag open. Out came a woman old enough to be Béia's grandmother. White roots showed through her thinning hair, dyed a fading ginger. She was skinny, her back curved. She wore a McDonald's uniform and visor and stood as if leaning on a counter, listening to a customer's order. In her tiny eyes, Béia recognized a melancholy for something lost, and the recognition made her recall that morning in this same hospital. The place had felt so different on Béia's day off. She remembered walking in silence back to the car next to her boyfriend. The little American woman in her hand glanced at her watch. Béia looked at the door leading back to the hospital. Work waited for her inside. She didn't want to waste her time being sad. Her palm itched beneath the lady's feet. She quickly put the woman in her mouth, avoiding her eyes. Once Béia's hands were empty, she finally got to scratch her itch, which had spread to both palms now. She rubbed her hands together one last time and returned to her shift.

In the emergency room, patients waited to the sound of the TV. Two angry blond women screamed about DACA on Fox News. In the storage room, Béia mixed the disinfectant with warm water and thought of the ultrasound morning again. The silence of the missing heartbeat. The nurse's face. How that face she'd seen so many times before in the hospital had changed after looking at the screen, avoiding Béia's gaze. Béia realized, staring at the nurse's profile in the darkened room, the face had been a shallow cutout, an outline without much depth. Before the ultrasound room, the nurse had been an extra, part of the scenery of Béia's life. But in that room, something sad and pitiful filled in the nurse's face, and she became something denser and harder to understand, another person. Béia thought of the neurological condition some people had where they could see but could not comprehend faces. She focused on the tension between the nurse's eyebrows. The nurse seemed to fail to contain an emerging frown. There was so much to the face, on the surface and underneath it. Béia felt sick and didn't want to think about what was happening. The nurse was going to get the doctor, she said, looking at Béia's boyfriend. No, there had been no blood until that morning, Béia told the doctor. "A silent loss," the moving mouth of the doctor said. Standing by the car afterward, she shrank away from her boyfriend's attempt to hug her. He talked about trying again, which made no sense. They had not tried anything in the first place. They had conceived without planning during their trip home to meet each other's families. She'd gotten sick early in their journey. They joked about her stomach having become Americanized, sensitive to the local food, and had not considered the minute possibility of the episode affecting her birth control. They didn't know if it'd happened in Bahia, where her parents lived, or São Paulo, where they visited his grandfather. The baby had been a little Brazilian gift they'd brought back with them without knowing. The suggestion of replacing it with something calculated in the New Jersey winter had struck her as repugnant. "Monstrous," said the woman on TV, as Béia rolled her bucket and mop out of the storage room and through the emergency waiting area.

Two days later, when she recovered her belongings from her cubby at the end of her shift, she saw missed calls from her ex-boyfriend. Shaking, she deleted his number. She cleared her call history so as not to find his traces there later. When she got home, her roommate seemed to be out, until she heard giggles coming from behind the closed door of her room and the voice of a man. Béia drank a glass of water and went to her bedroom. She put on her headphones. She didn't watch an episode of their show, in case the roommate wanted to see it later. She scrolled down her feed instead, pausing at each post she read to scratch her itching palms. But it was all too much, and she shut her laptop and lay in the darkness for hours until she finally fell asleep.

The following morning at work, she noticed something hardening in her hands, a thin scab trailing the M's on her palms. She put an orange cone where she'd been mopping, rested the mop and her bucket against the wall. The blond women on the waiting room TV talked about anchor babies. She went to wash her hands.

At lunchtime, she showed her palms to Patricia, who examined them closely, ran her fingers along each M, and frowned. She scratched at Béia's hands lightly with her fingernails, as naturally as if they were her own. She ended up scraping out of them a thin layer of something that looked like white cotton candy or a spiderweb. "Have you been working around any patients with skin diseases? Fungi?"

Béia shook her head, but they both knew there wasn't a way to know for sure.

"Maybe an allergy? With all these chemicals we deal with here, credo. Get it looked at, OK?"

After Patricia left, only a couple of minutes remained before the end of Béia's break. She hurried to the machine, more out of necessity than because she wanted to. She opened the bag on top of a table full of pharmaceutical pamphlets and distractedly looked at her left palm while her right hand reached inside the bag. She would make an appointment in a week or so if things didn't get better. When she looked at her right hand, a woman stood there with her back turned. Béia felt queasy. Something was wrong. The woman had tight shoulder-length curls, and the brown skin emerging from the uniform was like Béia's. The little body, still facing away, swayed back and forth. The woman held a mop. Béia's hands started to shake. Destabilized, the little woman stopped mopping for a second. She found her footing again and kept going, even as her floor trembled. The itching on Béia's hands was unbearable with the woman rubbing her mop on them. And Béia was terrified of seeing the woman's face. She tried to scratch around her. The woman began to turn. Béia threw her into her mouth and swallowed.

She woke up nauseated the following morning. Squinting at her with suspicion, Patricia asked if she was seeing anyone. "What are you up to, amiga? You can tell me. I'll do whatever I can, even harass the fucker to make sure he treats you right."

Béia swore it was impossible. There was no way she could be pregnant. Nothing had happened in months.

Patricia looked at her with pity, "Amiga, don't you think it's time? It would be good for you. Do you want me to introduce you to someone I know? There's this guy, we had a thing a while back. But we are good friends now. He's quite good in that department."

After Béia thanked her but refused, Patricia used her phone to diagnose her with possible gastritis. Rosa agreed. At home, Béia wanted to consult her roommate, but she almost never saw her these days. Either the apartment was empty, or her roommate was locked in her bedroom with her whispers, laughs, and the man's voice. She'd even heard them watching their 1960s series; the words were muffled, but she recognized the theme music. But they must have finished the series and seemed to have moved on to something else.

The first week of April, she tried to take a break from the machine again, but by then, she couldn't. She tried to hold out but usually gave in by around 2:00 P.M., 4:00 at the latest, while her apple slices and carrot sticks lay untouched in their ziplock bag. On Tuesday, she broke and ate a man wearing a suit, sputtering on his invisible phone, looking at what must have been a computer screen. She put him in her mouth, relieved he hadn't been familiar like the lady with the mop.

The weather was warmer. Béia's hands itched a little more with the heat. The next day, Patricia suggested Béia google rheumatoid arthritis. Rosa, who was now attending night school for nursing, disagreed. Despite her hands, Béia was happy that winter had dwindled down. Consistent with the seasonal change, Patricia made her annual announcement of her summer body regime:

"No beach-bud-fad-diet bullshit this year, amiga. Remember all that celery? Then all that kale? No, this year, I'll be legit. Not a diet. A lifestyle change. You know? Wholesome and shit. Are you with me?"

Béia laughed, shook her head.

"Don't get me wrong, you look great, Béia. But this isn't about looks. It's about an attitude to life, not just eating healthy, but being healthy. Though, of course, if I don't end up looking good in my bikini this year, I will hunt this Iara Rodrigues down. Or at the very least, I'll cancel my subscription to *Revista Caras*."

Béia wished to join Patricia. But the rest of the month, while Patricia did squats while heating her precisely portioned homemade soups, Béia ate so many others. Others whom at first she ingested without thinking but whose faces now came back to her, as she mopped or drove or lay in bed in the silence of her apartment, while her room-mate was out at her boyfriend's. There was the middle-aged delivery woman in her fraying brown jacket, balancing invisible boxes onto her back seat. The groceries cashier shuffling her weight from side to side as she stood, wiping a wisp of hair out of her eyes, before signaling for the next customer. The woman sitting cross-legged on the floor, aiming her invisible story at invisible children. Béia couldn't pinpoint when their faces had started coming to her like this. But now, when she went to the machine, she tried not to look too hard, not to linger.

So she wasn't sure whether the one she had on the last day of April actually looked like the patient who had slept in the room with the flowers, or whether she was misremembering. Had she imagined the tiny cannula underneath her nose, on her peaceful sleeping face? Béia swallowed her quickly. And when she went to the patient's room again the next day, of course, the patient was not there anymore. She had been gone, one way or another, for a couple of months. The bed was stripped, waiting for its next occupant. And the room was divided by a curtain now. On the other side, a patient snored softly. The TV showed the warehouses they had been showing lately, a wide shot outside the chain-linked fences. Then a closer shot of the inside. A child, dirty, about ten years old, holding the hand of a snotty toddler. Cut to the newsroom reporter. The patient's snoring stopped for a second, then started again. It was ten thirty. Béia left the room and headed to the machine.

A white man with gray hair and a thick gray beard came out. He appeared to hold a sign. He wore a MAGA hat and screamed, veins visible on his neck. And it was as if she were already ingesting the man's hatred. She wished he could see her, her mouth and teeth as they were about to crush him. She flicked his ear, and he waved his hand around the spot where she'd hit him, as if there'd been a mosquito buzzing around him, and then he screamed with more vigor. Béia's neck and jaw were rigid with anger. She shoved him into her mouth and bit hard. He cracked too easily, like a soft-shell crab. She realized she'd wanted real bones, breaking loudly between her teeth.

That night her apartment was empty again. She put on the series but couldn't concentrate, so she turned it off. In the dark, she remembered her ex's laugh when they'd been on the plane on the way to his grandpa in Brazil. She longed not only for him but for that whole moment. She didn't remember what they'd been laughing at. She remembered their hands held together, resting on her belly. She checked her phone. No messages. There were never messages now. Her room was even darker after her eyes adjusted to the bright screen when the light turned off. When she closed her eyes, she could see its afterimage, like a ghost's. And then the man with the MAGA hat. And the small snotty child on TV. She put a hand on her belly. Empty. Her emptiness continued into the emptiness of her room, that nothing in her and around her, like a thick syrup.

The next day, the first day of May, Béia had just put away her bucket and mop in the closet when she detected a smell coming from the break room with the microwave. It was faint at first, making her wonder if she was imagining it, but growing stronger as she walked toward the room. When she reached the threshold of the door, it hit her, disorienting her. She closed her eyes for a second, her hands leaning on the opening of the door. Musty, and sweet, organic, alive: both pleasant and unpleasant, like the body of someone you love can be, a smell that is real as itself, a smell that is home. Beans. And the bright bite of garlic. And beef. And onion.

"Come." Patricia held a pile of Tupperware containers and gestured with her head toward the corridor that led them to the small garden outside. "I brought us some real food."

They sat on a wide concrete planter. An airplane flew above. Then the sound subsided, and there was a birdcall, but she couldn't tell which; she still couldn't name the birds here. It was warm in the sun. Patricia opened the containers at her side and scooped out the still steaming rice, beans, fried yucca flour, tomatoes, and beef with onions. She arranged them carefully on one of those cafeteria paper plates. She gave the plate to Béia, a plastic fork and knife coupled together on the side.

Béia took her first bite. The food tasted so good, fresh and warm and full and dense. None of that light artificial crispiness of packaged food. And it was made with such care. And there was that warmth on her skin, still new at this time of the year.

Before preparing anything for herself, Patricia looked at Béia. "How are you, amiga?"

Béia looked back, her mouth still full. With her eyebrows dropped pitifully, she made a tiny shrug, her head turning into a short listless no. Patricia breathed in, looked ahead at a little brown bird that had descended into the planter across from them, and ran her hand on Béia's back. After swallowing, Béia filled herself with a staccato inhale that turned into a long sigh and began to cry. Patricia moved closer, and Béia lowered her head onto Patricia's shoulder. Patricia held Béia's hands and gently ran her fingers over her scars.

Only at the end of that day, she felt like going back to the machine again. It yielded a young woman with 1980s makeup, dressed up in a red dress and a matching red hat. She held a drink on her lap, alone, like someone had forgotten her, her expression so sad.

Béia didn't feel well the next day but came to work anyway. She didn't have many sick days left this year. The lines on her hands sometimes stung, like cuts under antibacterial spray. She was finally seeing someone about it after work that day. She still felt nauseated, like when she'd been pregnant. She stopped by the machine because the nausea was worse on an empty stomach.

She felt her forehead before bending to pick up the bag. She seemed to be running a fever. When she opened the bag, the contents did not come out straightaway. She turned the bag upside down over her open palm. The person who fell out was smaller than usual. The proportions were off. It was a small child, a girl, around two years old. Béia's skin color. Same hair. The little face, a mix: her ex-boyfriend's nose, Béia's eyes. Béia felt dizzy and lost her footing. She leaned on the wall. The child lifted her arms, the chubby fingers reaching, asking to be picked up. Béia was going to be sick. Her hands shook, and the baby and the package fell. She ran toward the bathroom. On the way, the TV woman said, "It's their fault for bringing them here." In the warehouse on the screen behind her, a chain-link fence surrounded children who slept like potatoes wrapped in aluminum foil. Béia barely made it to the toilet and threw up.

She went to the sink in a cold sweat and ran some water over her face. Something came from the lines on her hands. Sheets of thin metallic plastic hatched out. Looking in the mirror at the silver planes growing out of her palms, she thought of Wolverine, then Edward Scissorhands, the times she'd watched them dubbed in Portuguese in her living room as a child. She imagined herself on the TV, as her little child self watched. The plastic on her hands reflected the fluorescent hospital lights, like the sun on the surface of water. She remembered herself when she'd been even younger, walking by the ocean with her mother, the sunlight glinting on the sea, the white roses on the sand. In her memory, her mother was silhouetted by the bright sun. She thought of her baby. Now she knew her face.

She stumbled out of the bathroom and was able to reach the smaller storage closet where she put away the mop and bucket when she needed to take a break. She went in and did not turn on the light, not wanting to call attention to her presence. The plastic was growing longer, silver pouring from her hands to the ground. The plastic made a slippery sound as it slithered along the floor, then up around her, trailing the wall. She was surrounded by it, the never-ending ribbon of plastic, like the insides of thousands of oversized cassette tapes un-spooled around her, the silver thickening around her, making it hard to see anything beyond it. The plastic made a ceiling above her. She was losing her balance, pushed by the silver sheets closing in around her. She was falling, almost in slow motion, plastic ribbons cradling her slowly. She was lying on the ground, like the children sleeping in the gymnasium on TV, and her body was sealed into a bubble of plastic, still connected to her hands, like an umbilical cord.

Her nausea stopped. It was completely dark, but calm, comfortable now. She was warm, protected. Her body relaxed, and her head rested on a pillow of plastic. She was so tired. She'd been so tired, for so long.

She dreamed of her baby. In her dreams, they lay together under sheets of metallic plastic. They slept on their sides. She hugged her child, who was sometimes a baby, sometimes a toddler, sometimes a five-year-old. When her little girl moved or whimpered, she went "shhhhh, shhhhhh," and comforted her back to a quiet sleep.

But she woke up alone. She didn't know how long she'd been there. After so much silence, it was jarring to hear a disturbance outside her

package. There was a faint white noise of running circuitry, the sound
of coins going down a chute, and the machine gulping them down.
The outline of a coil of wire pressed against the plastic, and she felt the
surface move beneath her feet as her package was slowly pushed forward. She felt the edge of the shelf, and then the ground disappeared.
Her body floated to the top of the package as it fell, going down and
down, a free fall.

{　}

It was Tuesday evening again, workshop night, and the writer sat in the middle of the conference table, surrounded by other writers, or soon-to-be writers, which was how they all thought of themselves. Her role was to stay silent, while the other writers told her what was wrong with her story. The writers were gentle and kind, but their job was to find the problems so they could be fixed and the writer exculpated in the next draft. The exposed wood of the mid-century table was walnut. Article, she guessed. The writer didn't want to make eye contact with the others but didn't want to be rude. So she scribbled notes, like "make this clearer" on her manuscript, and "timeline" or "pg. 6" and "why her?" and "why now?" on the yellowed lined pages of her little notebook. It was pocket sized. Peter had brought it to her, from a conference goody bag. The workshop instructor at the head of the table said things like "interesting" and "can you expand on that?" and "hm."

She took a break from taking notes and stretched her fingers. The fellow curly-haired woman next to her smiled sympathetically. And then the writer was done. She thanked everyone and collected all the copies of her manuscript her classmates had annotated.

Everyone was going to the pub next door, but the writer couldn't. She had an early meeting the next morning at work. It was dark outside and drizzling. But her walk to the subway was not too long, and she would be okay. Cold, but not too cold. Early March, almost spring. That was one of her favorite things, spring. She'd grown up in uninterrupted good weather, and the first time she'd witnessed people sprouting at every outdoor space, patches of grass, benches, and cafes, stretching toward the sun. And she felt it too, in her own body, a happiness that felt physical, driven by her body more than her mind, a happiness for the simple, commonplace, and marvelous presence of warmth, the sun, and chlorophyll. Something she'd never experienced before she left, when those things were a constant, a pleasant background song.

The writer was also an immigrant. Sometimes, when the immigrant writer wrote, there was no migration in the story, and she wondered if there should be. Sometimes the immigrant writer wrote immigrant stories and wondered if she shouldn't. These were the kind of questions she talked about with the Devil.

In her story, she had only seen the Devil three times and spoken to him only once, that one night, but the writer still had conversations with him all the time in her head. Maybe it wasn't always the real thing, but it didn't feel completely unreal either. Like fiction, whether it was real in a literal sense was not the point. Though, at least with fiction, everyone was on the same page.

Not so with him, the Devil highlighted, appearing next to the writer with an umbrella that covered them both from the drizzle and the yellow streetlamp light. Or in autofiction, the Devil continued, indulging her, as this was also one of the subjects the writer liked to talk about with the Devil lately, though it was not of particular interest as a genre to him. He loved, craved, many kinds of stories. He searched and sometimes found what he was looking for in books, in late-night conversations in bars, in funerals, and in news reports. The soul, the words, the telling, he repeated. The writer and the Devil came to the subway entrance. He was not as interested in the literal physical reality of the story. As if to prove a point, he disappeared.

In the subway, one of the orange plastic seats was free, next to a lady carrying groceries. The writer placed the pile of annotated manuscripts on her lap. The full row of people across from her were looking at their phones. The subway smelled of damp hair and clothes, coming from her and maybe everyone else too. The lighting in the subway, yellow with a tinge of green, always made things seem hyperreal. Whenever she came into the subway from a dimly lit restaurant, party, the softly lit room where she had her workshop, it was like waking up from a dream.

Her feet ached. The woman next to her rummaged, looking for something inside one of the paper grocery bags. She gave up and started looking at her phone too. The writer was bad at social media. Anytime she posted anything, it felt like the words were not her own. Like a multiple-choice test or possession. Like she herself was also a device, channeling somebody else's words. Even when she agreed, it felt as if the words and the thoughts were not hers. And sometimes things were so obviously bad or wrong, it confused her. And sometimes it was hard to think about what was right if you allowed for people and things to be partially correct and partially wrong or unknown or unknowable. And sometimes it was also hard to know what was real. Not like ghosts or witches or the Curupira. But just in the simplest surface sense: Were the statistics behind the infographic real? Were they outrageously misleading? The writer sometimes researched. But halfway through, her sense of duty faltered. Was her lifetime enough to go on chases after every whim of the algorithm? The algorithm was always hungry.

The woman with the grocery bags got up to get off at the next stop, revealing the Devil, just two seats down. He paused his reading of the *New York Post* and looked at her with a mixture of love and pity, like you might look at a sleeping puppy as it moves its little paw, the little nose sniffing as it chases god knows what in its dreams.

The writer adjusted her manuscripts on her lap. The top page was dotted with raindrops.

Sometimes she wondered if she was writing what was expected of her. Or if she prevented herself from writing things that were true and she wanted to say, only because it was expected. She did think of her family, and all their skins were such a beautiful brown in the summer, and she loved mangoes, especially the ones she found hanging from tall loaded trees all over her hometown, free for anyone who wanted them, and she loved the music, etc., etc. And she didn't feel welcome here, etc., etc. But she also spent long stretches without thinking about the fact she was an immigrant at all. She didn't talk to the Devil about how she didn't think only immigrant thoughts. He already knew.

The Devil folded his newspaper. He smiled at her and pointed at the door. It was her stop. She gathered her manuscripts and headed home.

# IDLE HANDS

Dear Amanda,

Thanks for sharing your draft of "Idle Hands" with us.

It was nice seeing a story with some real people in it this time (the first of your stories in this workshop with no writers). So far, it is my favorite of your submissions, and I feel it could be just the beginning of work that has a more universal appeal.

The Walmart-like setting is interesting, it evokes a place that is immediately familiar. I very quickly see the large warehouse space, the plain, polished concrete floors, the repeated pattern of fluorescent lights high above. I liked that description of the symmetry of the shelves containing a cacophony of bright plastic products and packaging. It got me thinking of the incongruity of all the disparate logos and colors, somehow contained within the regularity of the corridors and the repeating store signs ("always in that navy blue") labeling each section, and that reassuring repetition of the "Everyday Low Price" mantra. I wonder though if people who had been working there for a while would really pause at that stage in their employment to notice such things (wouldn't it all become familiar and somewhat invisible to them?). But I do think this idea of an organized chaos is interesting, and could be a nice metaphor for the necessary work still to be done in this story:

maybe finding a more structured way to present the many threads you have here might be beneficial.

One way you could give this story a tighter structure might be using the days leading up to Black Friday as a counter (remember how well the countdown to the Halloween party worked in Jennifer's story?). But I think you can make more use of the countdown as a frame as well as a way to create some time pressure. If you do that, maybe you can get rid of the memos. I think they don't add much to the main storyline and feel a little awkward, like an author's attempt to be quirky, rather than an organic part of the story.

Maybe instead, you could use that memo space to develop the relationship between Maggie and Matt, which is more promising. There are a few nice moments (even if the prose and details could be tightened), like when Maggie shares her soggy sandwich with Matt. Just when I start to feel there is potential for something, we trail off onto the memo business. Maybe spend more time on these scenes between the two of them instead. Their relationship is the heart of the story.

I wasn't sure about the cat. It didn't seem that believable to me. It felt cliché somehow (black cat, the bodega cat, etc.). I have seen that before. I doubted Walmart (or its proxy) would allow a black cat to be hanging out in the storage room like that. And that scene where Emanuel thinks the cat is talking to him, well, I think you were going for humor? But I am not sure it lands.

Of the minor characters, I liked Mr. D best, but I do wonder, other than functioning as a sounding board to the two love birds, does he really have a significant role in the narrative?

I hope I am not being too critical here, just trying to help. I am interested to see if the group agrees with me on this one. I do hope you keep working on this type of story (perhaps a more fruitful mode to pursue than those "writers-thinking-about-ghosts" style stories). You seem to be figuring some things out here.

Best of luck,

Joanne

--------------------------------------------------------------------

Workshop — "Idle Hands"

Critique by Paula Francis

Summary as I see it:

In "Idle Hands" a cast of workers in an unnamed large department store prepare for the upcoming Black Friday sale. Over the course of several days, interpersonal relationships develop and tensions between the base-level associates and the middle managers increase, as they try to follow the "suggestions" sent via memorandum by an invisible upper management. There is a budding romance between two associates (Matthew and Maggie), as well as a contentious friendship between Emanuel and Clark. The latter culminates in a tense disagreement, soon before the doors open for the Black Friday event. Possibly, this disagreement was "the last drop," so to speak, leading Clark to go ahead and execute his plan to do a gruesome art installation involving goldfish (despite Mr. D having tried to gently dissuade him of his plans or was he? Not 100% on that one). The story ends with customers pushing on the doors from the outside, as they count the seconds for the Black Friday sale to start.

Critique:

Some of the interactions between Clark and Emanuel (and of both characters separately with Mr. D) were effective. In particular, the conversation on the logic of placements in the personal hygiene section (which had to remain hypothetical, given those decisions were made in a corporate setting far away from this local store), and the ongoing discussion on whether or not Clark had free will. Clark and Emanuel's mutual decision that they should resolve their differences in "a civilized fistfight off-premises" also worked. So did the challenging (impossible?) task of finding a time when both Emanuel and Clark were off duty to schedule the fight. That shared purpose effectively gave the story the opportunity to have them get along better for a while, and end up replacing the fight that failed to materialize by a plan to get high in the storage room together (I wonder if that had been Mr. D's goal all along or if that was unintentional. Perhaps that could be made clearer).

Mr. D's mediation throughout was also interesting. We get the feeling that he is an old wise man type, having worked there for the longest time (by "not getting too many raises and keeping a low profile,") and has a somewhat "mystical" vibe ("Matt tried not stare at his eyes, which were of slightly different colors: one honey brown, almost green, and the other darker"; "when he turned around, there was Mr. D, standing there, ready for the question"; "The fine hairs on the nape of Maggie's hair stood up. It was not what Mr. D said, but that moment when he looked at her with his mismatched eyes. It was then she knew she would do it and it felt like she were just performing a role that had been decided for her somewhere far away, before the whole thing had even begun"; and "but Mr. D was calm, a faint smile on his face, a trace of a hum only Matt could hear, as if he already knew what would happen when the doors opened, and all would be as it should, according to some grand plan only Mr. D knew"; etc.).

The main issue here is that there are too many characters and storylines for such a short story, making it so you don't have enough space to develop any of them fully. I think you should focus on the Emanuel-Clark thread, which would make the goldfish scene even more impactful. Minimize the role of the other characters or scratch them all together. Keep Mr. D., but maybe don't involve him as much.

---

Lovely Amanda,

I really enjoyed reading your story! I loved the shenanigans of Emanuel and Clark! That scene where they are high taking inventory and Clark passes out and Emanuel talks to the cat! So fun! Such a barely hidden bromance with those two, you can tell that they secretly adore each other! I also love how everyone keeps chasing the cat and never manages to catch it. And the thing between Maggie and Matt is sweet!

I just wanted a lot more. More about these characters, their wants and desires, their fears. What were they like before the prep for Black Friday began? Especially Maggie. I don't really get a sense of who she is so I don't fully understand her decision in the end. Also, a bit more development there would make her relationship with Matt even more touching.

Also, maybe some of the observations on the store (the setting, the procedures, etc.) could be thought from Matt's pov (since he is new and thus more prone to noticing things). Some of that can also be delivered to him as part of his orientation (along with those hilarious right-to-work videos), or by Mr. D as he is always sharing his bits of wisdom anyway (btw, I love how there is this possibility that Mr. D is totally sly, and sometimes uses reverse psychology! He is a lot of fun. Maybe give him more space on the page?).

The other major thing for me was the goldfish stuff :-O. Maybe a little too gruesome? I know we don't see anything happen on screen . . . but still. We kind of know that when the Black Friday crowd comes in, someone is bound to turn one of the blenders on. Too much, no?

But still, this was a super fun read. You have improved so much as a writer even within the weeks of this workshop! And I am sure you will only get better as you continue developing! Cannot wait to see where you take things.

<3

Jennifer

P.S.: I think this is your last story for this session and I wanted to say it has been an absolute pleasure! You are such a sweetie and always so supportive! Thank you so much for your advice on my last story. I wanted to let you know that it was picked up by *Ploughshares*! I submitted it before workshop, so I didn't get the chance to make any of all those changes generously offered by the class (The *Ploughshares* editors only made two changes, which were typos, lol! I was so embarrassed), but still! Thanks for all the suggestions! I may announce it in class, but I wanted you to be the first to know.

---

Hi Amanda,

Here is my critique of "Idle Hands."

<u>What is working</u>: The setting (Walmart provides a familiar and contained universe for the story. We feel trapped, like the characters). The subtle love story (they are cute/sweet . . . though maybe try turning the heat up between the two of them and see what happens (e.g. what if they finally got down in the storage room? And what if Emmanuel and Clark walk in right then and finally manage to get the black cat? I don't know, I think it could be interesting to consider such what-ifs). Clark's descent into derangement was also great (the whole thing from him finally stealing the goldfish to his speech (internal or to Mr. D? not clear) to the placing of the fish in the appliances).

<u>What could be worked on:</u> the memos, the veiled commentary on
the anti-union propaganda (which is not really surprising given the
Walmart setting), some of the sober discussions between Emanuel and
Clark. I.e., the political and philosophical stuff. Those sections are too
abstract and essayistic. It feels as if there is an agenda there. Maybe
stick to the sensorial/concrete and either imply or let go of some of
the more abstract stuff.

> Cheers,
> Mitch

---

Hey Amanda,

Thanks for your story. There were some things I really enjoyed here:

- The contrast between the tenderness between Maggie and
  Matt and the procedural nature of tasks required for Matt's
  orientation
- Little fun details, like how someone surrounded one of the
  memos in Chiquita Banana stickers; the old abandoned
  bashed up parrot piñata, which appears to have hung in the
  back room from the beginning of time (does the cat live in
  there?)
- The sense of precarity in the workers (e.g. the stories about
  people who had been fired, etc.)
- The way in which everyone is immersed in that corporate
  culture and can't help but buy into it at some level, even if
  made skeptical by all they witness (e.g. "Maggie turned the
  slip of paper around and placed it back on the shelf, face
  down. She did have hope, despite herself. It had to be possible, at least for some of them. Her managers all had started

out just like her. Look at them now, she thought. She'd make it. And when she got there, she would do things differently. Her friends might become disappointed in her now. But she would make it up to them later, and, in the end, they would be grateful for what she had to do.")

One thing that I am wondering about though, is the position/authority of the author in regards to this setting/population. Coming from a small town where Walmart is the main employer, the setting and the preoccupations of the characters here don't sit quite right with me. It's more like what a liberal coastal city person concerned with labor relations, who may have visited a Walmart once or twice would imagine, rather than a real place. There is some care and interest for the people, but they don't feel genuine. I wonder if this is the author's story to tell.

I think to address that last point, you could try to recast these ideas into a situation that is more familiar to you (which may be hard/not possible in this particular story). If you are going to stick to the current events and setting, maybe do a little more research on the place and population it portrays. Also consider having a first-person narrator for one draft, just as an exercise. It might force you to embody and empathize with one of the characters and handle their concerns a little more carefully.

J.P.

-----

Dear Amanda,

It was so cool to get to read your story after talking about it the other night (the hangover was totally worth it. So glad we decided to go out after being so freaked out by *Häxan*. Someone should have warned us ;-)).

I enjoyed many moments of the story. For example, the part where Emanuel and Clark seem to finally be in potential trouble for their mischief and are considering the possible consequences. I loved that Mr. D's deliberations about their situation reproduced a cool version of the prisoner's dilemma and how in the end, they both end up agreeing that they can't trust each other and conclude that the only logical option is to choose option 1, where both tell on each other and proclaim their own innocence, even if that is a sub-optimal strategy. That resonates nicely with both the anti-union and the free-will discussions that come earlier.

I love the echoes of our favorite book (which I was delighted to find out in our conversation the other night). I wonder if more could be made of it. For example, maybe the workers can organize an impromptu Thanksgiving snack dinner (since they have to miss most/all of the holiday) (cf. Woland's ball in the novel, it could be somehow "hosted" by Mr. D and Maggie). I don't know, just more little things like that, as the reference is maybe too subtle right now. I did think about it more since we talked and you are right, the whole thing can be very interesting. I particularly like the fact that in both your story and M&M, characters talk themselves into not seeing whatever contradicts the ideology they are surrounded by, though the ideologies themselves are (somewhat) reversed (atheism/casual Christianism, communism/capitalism, etc.). I do wonder though, if I can really access all of that on the page. I feel like what I am seeing here is partially (or entirely) only visible because we talked about this explicitly the other night. Something to think about.

Speaking of the Devil, a totally random, but maybe helpful reference: I am reading this book (not a novel, an academic work on political theology). It compares the neoliberal worldview to a theology and talks about how the idea of freedom is used to assign the source of evil to individual choices (i.e., we are all given just enough choice to be deemed responsible for the bad stuff). The author also has another one on the history of the concept of the Devil that is on my to-read pile. Both may be interesting reads given what we talked about the other day.

Let's grab another beer and talk more about it soon?

Love,

Erin

P.S.: Not sure what to expect from the class discussion. But, I'll pre-emptively say, given what I witnessed in the discussion of ghosts last time: take what certain other readers suggest with a grain of salt.

-------------------------------------------------------------------------------

Amanda's Story ("Idle Hands") — Critique by Robert (Nice to see your work again!)

The shy romance is touching and Emanuel and Clark are funny at times (I chuckled at that black cat scene). But here is what I thought: most of the characters/relationships feel gestural to me. There is a seed of something interesting there, but it feels schematic. I think what's happening is that this story is mainly interested in ideas rather than the particulars of these characters. But because you tried to give them some meat, but didn't go all the way, the story is hovering somewhere in between: not fully developing the characters nor the ideas.

But that is not to say that all is lost! I feel that the solution is in there, staring us in the face (just like Mr. D when he is being creepy!): the memos. The memos (including the ten "friendly suggestions") were my favorite part of this piece. As they are, they provide a good way for upper management (who don't belong in this place, different social class, reality, etc.) to dictate things without taking over the story. But I also like the idea of having this artifact as a potential mediator for the ideas. (Plus, consider there must be a reason why epistolary writing consistently pokes its head out and remains popular over the years.) What would happen if the whole thing happened in memos? You may have to shelve some of the threads (which I think you should anyway), but it could be interesting and may solve some of your problems. Also, have you read *Fakes*?

Some good kernels in here. Looking forward to seeing where you take it.

Thanks!

---

Dear Amanda,

I like how grounded this seemed compared to your other stories. This kind of thing may be something you keep working on, even if you end up going back to that meta-stuff you like. I am a big believer of learning the rules before you break them. And I think you may be taking steps toward learning the rules here.

Having said that, I was still a little confused during much of the story. I wasn't sure about the function of the memos and all those conversations about hypotheticals. But most of all, I just wasn't sure what was physically happening a lot of the time. Was that because Emanuel and Clark were high? That doesn't quite jibe with my experience (what drugs are they on exactly?). Did the cat talk? Was the business with the goldfish real? How did that work exactly? Where is all of that taking place within Walmart? I think the common theme here is that in revision you should take a look at how you handle both space and time.

What is really sticking is Maggie and Matt, which I enjoyed. That's where the language is naturally giving more sensory detail. But I also wondered: who is the audience for this story?

I like Mr. D. He is cute and likable and, despite my realistic fiction preferences, I love a good old Devil figure in a story. I wonder if more could be done with him though. If given a little bit more room, he could steal the show (in a good way). But even in its current form, it made me wonder: if Mr. D is the Devil, are the Waltons God?

Best regards,

Ana

{ }

The streets were empty and quiet. They didn't leave the house much, didn't see anyone but coworkers on Zoom. So many people were dying, and their sadness felt unjustified, unearned, wrong. Yet they were sad. And Peter got them a kitten. It was fluffy and black, and when he arrived, he fit in the writer's hand. They called him "B" because they enjoyed being cryptic and because they tried to dress him up as a bee for Halloween, bee stripes cut out of a used manila envelope. It had only been a few weeks, but the writer loved him already, which was why she let B take the queen now. B pawed the piece across the light wooden floor. As it spun and slid under a dining chair, B arched his back and jumped backward, his little tail pointing up. He had just walked through the chess game she and Peter played slowly on the coffee table. It took them days to finish a game. The writer made her moves between calls in the morning. She flipped the quarter next to the board back so that George Washington would let Peter know it was his move. He made his when he walked by on the way to the kitchen with his empty mugs. Or before putting on his mask and going out to pick up the groceries, which he'd done just ten minutes ago.

The writer took the mug of hot water from the microwave and stirred in the instant coffee. They were out of the good stuff and almost out of toilet paper. There was no toilet paper, anywhere. The writer worried about Peter at the supermarket. But what could they do? She thought she had been winning the game B destroyed, but she wasn't sure. The different games were merging in her head. The pieces were scattered around the edges of the board, except for the white king, still standing in place, and the white queen, lying under the chair. The writer took a sip of her coffee and began placing the pawns back in their places. She felt the Devil next to her. B noticed him too. He abandoned the queen and walked past the writer toward the Devil. B rubbed against him, as if greeting an old friend. The Devil smiled and ran his hands on the kitten's back. B purred.

The Devil looked at the pawns lined up on the board; his smile faded a little. So many pawns lined up, identical as if they were a reflection multiplied in a corner of mirrors. They stood in oblivious pride, ready to be disposed of, one by one. As the writer put back the towers and the knights, she told the Devil about seeing the US and Brazil together at the top of the list that morning. A list of countries ranked by number of deaths, numbers hard to imagine or put in perspective. She had thought of the line separating the two countries as the boundary of a perverse mirror. The president in Brazil had been called "Trump of the Tropics." The two men acted so similarly, a franchise. As she'd looked at the list, the numbers, she could hear the voice of the Brazilian president say "the little cold," as he called it. The Devil nodded as he put back the bishops. He looked at the pieces on the board, mirroring each other, and said it was always difficult. Of course, he had seen this—pandemics, evil, powerful men—all before. He said it didn't make it any less tragic and said sorry. The writer asked if he could do anything. The Devil said what he could do himself was always very little, unlike what others could do using his name. He bent over, picked up the queen from under the chair, and handed her to the writer. The writer held it for a second, feeling the warmth dissipating in her hands. She put the queen back in her place. When she looked up, the Devil was gone. B was curling up on the corner of the green sofa. On the board, the central pawn had advanced. The coin flipped to the eagle with her spread wings.

# RENT

Miki had told Tê the piano was haunted. Miki could hear it in the reverberation behind the low keys and the strident leftover in the highs. But Tê knew nothing about pianos. She opened its cover and exposed the keys. It grinned like a dog. She pressed down, her ten fingers stretched apart. It sounded sinister, she gave Miki that.

Jason had left, his room was empty, and the envelope he promised to slip under her door, with the rent money, had never appeared. When he moved in, he had agreed to bring a deposit, but the day he moved in (that strawberry-blond hair, that pointy nose, that collar neatly tucked into his cardigan), asking had seemed rude and unnecessary. And there was the piano. Tê had never thought she would live with a piano. Now it sat underneath a pile of unpaid utility bills. Tê stuck her fingers under its jaw, leaned back, and put the weight of her body into the pull. It didn't move.

Later she found out Jason had told Miki the piano belonged to his dead aunt. He claimed she had gone mad after a failed love affair with a married man. Supposedly, he had loved her, but he was related to royalty and could not face the scandal of leaving his wife. Jason's aunt had played their song until her fingers bled and became deformed with calluses. She drank poison and kept playing until her dead torso fell on the keys, producing a final, perfect harmony.

Just the kind of story that would turn Miki on.

Tê brought her nose close to the piano's shiny brown surface. But it didn't smell like anything. Jason's cologne smelled nice, like flowers about to rot and wood.

To Tê, Jason had talked about his classical training, the strict private French tutor who'd hit his knuckles with a ruler, the neglect of his rich parents, his decision to make it on his own, not a cent from his trust fund. It turned out he had been sleeping with Miki too and, mostly likely, also with Angela, who had not paid her last month's rent either and who, by the looks of it, had run off with him.

Tê had tried to sell the piano on Craigslist. Then she'd tried to give it away for free. Turned out, it was worthless. A piece of crap all along. That was what made her mad. She had not been able to tell the difference. Still couldn't. The piano sounded fine to her.

She kicked it. A pressure escaped her with the thump, like it did with the best of sighs. She kicked it again. She kicked it, and it groaned faint notes to her, like warm whispers in her ear.

Miki came out of her room, rubbing her eyes. The piano was slightly crooked against the wall. It had moved, even if just a few centimeters. And there was a nice crack on the panel.

Tê went to the basement and came back with a hammer for herself, a frying pan for Miki.

"She spoke to me in a dream. This," Tê murmured, "is how we free her."

{            }

In the beginning, the virus traveled on our hands, and it covered all our surfaces. But before that, the virus was poisoned wells, punishment from God, bad air, witchcraft, the fruits of the wickedness of the Devil. And the virus was in the fleas. And the fleas were in the rats. Now people wiped each green pepper and tomato ordered online, careful so they would not touch the counter before being disinfected. And people were urged not to wear ill-fitting masks, and then they were urged to wear any mask, imperfect as it might be. They were not to touch their faces, not to touch one another. Clean their hands. Sing "Happy Birthday" twice.

The virus was out there, its potential presence an invisible film covering everything, filling the empty streets. The writer was washing her hands in her bathroom. Her face looked tired under the greenish-yellow fluorescent lights, dark circles under her eyes; she had not slept. She had not worn makeup for months. The writer thought of the lion in the movie *12 Monkeys*, which she'd first watched before she spoke English, in a New York far away in time and space. She thought of the lions in front of the public library in the New York that was now her home.

She thought of the fake pictures going around—animals taking over cities, dolphins in Venice—and the real pictures of the Chernobyl Exclusion Zone. The animals and the green forests growing on the ruins or the brutalist architecture that reminded her of the apartment where she'd grown up. She thought of the streets just outside, the makeshift graves. She remembered the headline she'd seen earlier that day: the closing of the restaurants had led the city rats to be "starving, angry and cannibalistic." She continued to wash her hands.

The writer had been reading about the Devil before all this. And now she alternated between the history of the idea of the Devil and the history of how we understood viruses. New understanding turned what had once been a fact into fiction. Just outside the bathroom, her books piled on her desk. She thought them dirty. She wanted to wipe them, like they'd wiped everything in the beginning. The Devil must have known the virus was on the fleas then, and he knew about whatever they were doing wrong now. She had lost count of the "Happy Birthday"s. She paused the scrubbing and stared angrily at the mirror, where she knew the Devil would be, standing behind her. She asked him if he had known, about the fleas, about the rats—had he tried to tell anyone? The Devil didn't have to answer. He knew then and he knew now. People never knew how to listen. The writer found herself angrier with the Devil than with God, if there was one. Naturally, as intended, the Devil said, or maybe she thought it herself. Wasn't that the whole point of the Devil? Someone for you to get angry at. And she was angry. So many people had died. So many people were dying. The Devil broke the rules. The Devil was already damned. Why didn't he do anything? Why didn't he do something now?

How many happy birthdays? Peter's birthday was coming soon, in a couple of weeks. The writer tried to hold on to her anger, because once it was gone, there would be something else. She wanted to go into the room, to comfort and take care of him. But Peter had begged her not to come in. She needed to be well, outside the room, to take care of him. Her anger was spilling through her fingers. She couldn't hold on to it. What did it say about her, with everything that had gone on, that was always going on all the time, before this, before Peter got it, the present, and history, and everything, that she only got angry with the Devil for not stopping things now? The Devil moved to comfort her, to touch her shoulder, but stopped himself. She turned to the Devil. The Devil was so sorry. Then something moved on the ground just behind them. A little paw slipped through the crack at the bottom of the door, a little comma moving over the old beat-up white tiles. B was going to do it again; he had learned how to do it a couple of days ago. It was like magic. He started squeezing through the opening under the door. He could fit into the tiniest crack. His head squeezed through, followed by his whole body. And he was in. She laughed, despite herself; it looked so ridiculous. And her anger was gone. She sat on the floor and picked up the kitten; her laugh morphed into a sob. She sat and stroked B until it was gone. Then the writer got up. She walked past the closed door of their bedroom and went back to her desk.

{     }

The writer thought about the rat in her story:

~~The rat comes and talks to the man.~~

~~The rat talks to the man. It turns out the rat is the spirit of the man's dead father.~~

~~After the man decides to throw out his TV, the rat broadcasts the news to him.~~

~~The man becomes the rat.~~

~~The rat eats the man.~~

~~The man eats the rat.~~

~~The rat is starving, angry, and cannibalistic.~~

~~The rat is the Devil.~~

~~The rat never comes.~~

~~The rat is just a rat.~~

# PORCELAIN

It was Saturday again, and Bernard had ended up deciding against going out. He had gotten close: his navy sweater buttoned up, his hair combed. But his moccasins lay empty by the door. Trader Joe's would be full of people and their children, getting under things, running by, unnervingly close as he reached for his jar of green olives. Bernard decided to brew himself some tea. He was thinking now of that story he'd heard once on NPR again, about a guy in Brooklyn who'd found a rat in his toilet. Apparently, it had climbed the pipes, and when this man walked in, there it was, squeaking up at him. He had dreamed of a rat, that night after he heard the story. In his dream, the rat rested on his pillow. It sat next to Bernard as he did his crossword puzzle. Bernard didn't remember the rest. Maybe there had been nothing else. When he'd woken up, everything had looked as it always had.

At work he almost told Valeria the story, when they both stood by the coffee maker, waiting for their cups to fill. But he had trouble thinking of a way to transition into it after their usual greeting. They asked each other, "How are you?" They said, "Good." Bernard liked Valeria, though they never talked. The people in the office were cordial enough, and he didn't terribly mind going to work. Though sometimes he imagined what it would be like to work somewhere else. Maybe a suit-and-tie kind of place. Bernard didn't wear a suit and tie. He did wear button-up shirts and slacks. There wasn't much reason for dressing up. It was not like he could upset the paperwork by not being presentable while processing parking permits. It's not like many people saw him there behind the piles of paper on his old-fashioned mahogany-veneer desk, his office all the way back, far from the public-facing counters. Other than Valeria, sometimes Bernard bumped into Charlie when he had to take something to the mail room. Sometimes one of the two clerks came all the way back to Bernard's office in search of something they could use to prove a constituent complaint unfounded. But such occurrences were rare. The last time it had happened, Bernard sifted through his papers slowly to stretch time, as he didn't know when something like that would come by again. Bernard wished he could work in tech, in one of those industrial lofts. Giant windows, a foosball table, people bouncing in red, yellow, and blue medicine balls, a guy on a standing desk high-fiving all coworkers hello as he coded a friendly artificial intelligence. Bernard tried to picture himself joining that Thursday happy hour across the road from the place he sometimes got milk when running low between grocery trips. He imagined inviting Valeria and Charlie to happy hour. What would he talk about? He decided happy hour was not for him.

Though he could be wrong. By now he knew people were sometimes bad at predicting how different situations might make them feel. For example, he'd thought he would not miss Wanda when she left. He was, in a way, looking forward to it. That had been the most foolish part. Of course, he was miserable. But that had been decades ago, and he didn't miss her anymore now. He would even return the tea set she'd inherited from her mother, but there was no occasion for it anymore, and Bernard guessed she was also used to not having it by now. Bernard used the set for tea on the weekends. He liked how fancy it felt. He liked the contrast of the small purple and pink flowers with the white porcelain. He liked the fading golden rim around the cups' lips. And the saucers. He'd never otherwise have bothered with them, but he was glad he had them. He'd ended up buying himself the almond biscotti he was having right now, to have something to rest in the saucer. And for that, he was grateful. Wanda had called him "Bernie." But he hadn't been called that for a long while now. Things that happened a long time ago could feel ancient and recent at the same time. In any case, he was also glad he'd no longer been known as "Bernie" by the time that man from Vermont was showing up everywhere. That might have been awkward. Maybe there would have been jokes at work, and he would not have known how to respond. Either way, the signs with the man's name spread around his neighborhood during the primaries—"Bernie," "Bernie," "Bernie"—had made him think of Wanda. Sometimes that was not a bad thing. Sometimes it was not so nice.

But Wanda was another story. The story Bernard had in mind was the one about the Brooklyn guy and the rat. Maybe that was what he would tell Charlie and Valeria at happy hour. The man's toilet must have been closed when the rat showed up; Bernard knew because he remembered the man saying he saw the rat after lifting the lid. He had to have put the tip of his thumb right under the toilet lid, lifted its full weight with one hand at the same time as his other hand pinched his zipper between thumb and index finger. Right when his zipper hit the end of its track and the lid clicked against the toilet tank, he saw the rat surrounded by white-glazed porcelain and water. It looked back at him with a wet expression of animal incomprehension, which partially mirrored his. Though his confusion was human, which was more pitiful, as humans like to think of themselves as an understanding species. He closed and held the lid down, feeling a little disgusted to touch it, the rat in such proximity on the other side. He waited for the thump of the rat jumping against the lid, trying to push it open, but there was nothing. He flushed the toilet and waited. Nothing but water. He flushed it again. Then again and again until it sounded like there was not enough water left. The handle offered no resistance to his turns, as if it had given up, so he sat on the closed toilet as more water trickled in. He waited enough time for the tank to refill, then flushed it decidedly, hoping it would be the last time. He heard the shush of the water coming down, then swirling, and then the final swallow. He wondered if the sound was obstructed by the rat, but he couldn't tell. He sat quietly on the lid for a time, no longer disgusted to be sitting there, having gotten used to the idea of the rodent. He didn't know for how long he sat. He was alone and had left his phone in the kitchen. Time was impossible to hold on to without a means to measure it, contain it.

The man opened the bowl and found the rat was still there and felt paralyzed by the impossibility of those dark gelatinous eyes looking at him. The wet fur was stuck to its head in a way that made it look angry. It moved, gathering itself in a spring of muscle and dark fur. Then it leaped. The man, the hipster from NPR, pushed the lid back down, cursing himself for having opened it. But it was too late. The top half of the rat—the front paws, with their fingers and long nails, its triangular head, and the teeth, which were animal and toddler and old man—was already out of the bowl. Even with the man holding the lid down, the rat was perplexingly compressing its body and pouring itself out farther. He'd heard about how rats could do this before, but the sight of it was terrifying. The man moved along the curve of the lid as far as possible and pressed down harder against the resistance of the rat's pulpous mass, cringing at the thought of hurting it, but not knowing what else to do. He didn't break the rat in two and managed to stop it from moving out farther. He stretched himself enough to get his girlfriend's hairbrush from the sink and used it to try and push the rat back in. But it was useless. So he just sat next to the rat, who breathed with some difficulty through its sepulchral open mouth.

It was then the man stopped telling the story. He said hurriedly that there had been no way out. He had to kill it. This hipster man from Brooklyn, who'd never killed anything and sounded like a decent-enough guy, had to do it. He said, "It was awful," and Bernard was thankful he didn't say more.

Bernard would not have killed the rat. He'd have sat with it, on top of the toilet. He would have kept it around until it got tired of him. Bernard wondered how it would feel to have another living thing appearing here just like that. It was raining now, Bernard's tea was cold, and he had to pee. He got up and walked to the bathroom. He wished he'd closed the lid last time to delay what he could see so plainly now: the white bowl empty, alone underwater.

{   }

The writer wanted to write a story about a demon who lived in someone's computer and who turned them into a cat anytime they went on a Zoom call. The character was angry when they saw on the news a lawyer had gone viral because he couldn't figure out the Zoom settings and had to defend a case as a cat. But the lawyer in real life could have turned off the effect anytime, if he knew where to click. While the character in the story worked in tech and knew what they were doing. They could not turn the cat face off because they were cursed.

The writer wanted to write another story about a woman whose partner, or child, or best friend, was afflicted by an illness. The main character would search the internet, scouring WebMD and online forums. She would buy herbs from suspicious websites. She would try traditional cures from her homeland. Nothing worked. Until she found this one strange forum, with quirky nice people. A woman would post asking the main character to do something, a combination of clicks and placing a mixture of herbs in her dying houseplant, and immediately, the houseplant would perk up and flourish. The main character would start frequenting the forum, as the relationship with the partner, child, or friend changed. Or didn't really change—something that had already been there, but hidden, would be revealed. That revelation, whatever it might be, would be the "snow falling faintly and faintly falling" moment. As a background thread, the conversations in the forums would sound a little like those in writing workshops. It would become clear with time the people in the forum were witches. The story would be called "Craft." The writer thought of these stories, trying to distract herself. But she couldn't write them now. She was too worried about Peter.

# HEAVEN, HELL, AND PURGATORY

## HEAVEN

She didn't know for sure how long she had been in the all-inclusive resort, which was also heaven, she'd concluded somewhat recently or a long time ago. Her awareness of being there had been gradual, she thought: a sensation after a dream you can't remember, then the memory of the dream, then the dream itself, then a dream that becomes lucid. She never did wake up, though her experience of the place became more coherent. Now there was the beach, the bright morning, the sand, the twinkling reflection on the water, slightly overexposed. The light, always familiar, like memories of summer beach vacations in movies or heaven in movies, when the main character was greeted by God dressed in a white suit. But there was no god for her. Though she was wearing white, like you did for the New Year in the country where she came from, which was not the country where she'd lived when she'd lived. Here she took walks on the beach, lay on the lounge chairs, lined up for meals from the buffet. Though she wasn't sure she had ever lined up behind anyone, couldn't remember anyone but herself. And her hunger had been faint, partially theoretical, compared to her memory of past hungers. Past hungers from when she'd been alive somewhere else (where?), someplace other than heaven.

When she settled on "heaven," it wasn't because she had entirely ruled out other possibilities. It was that now she sensed the truth was less categorical, more a matter of settling somewhere along a statistical continuum. Ruling things out didn't seem completely necessary. Both that new understanding of truth and the diminished status of her hunger came from her improbable existence away from a body. A real body, that is, because in this heaven, she was still her, with her hands, hair, feet, and legs, though she had not seen a mirror in a while. She held her hands out in front of her, thinking maybe they would become transparent, like that guy in a movie she'd loved as a child whose name or plot she could not remember. But she only looked at her hands briefly, distracted by the white sand behind them. She drew spirals with her index finger, then picked up a fistful and let it escape slowly. She could feel the sand, but faintly, as if it were the memory of sand. Her thinking escaped her like that in this place. But she didn't mind.

Thinking of other options for where she was was not as pleasant. But she still did. At first, out of habit, she considered maybe this was a real place. But there were no bills, access wristbands, additional tour offers, reservations, emails from work (what work did she do?). So maybe, it was something else. Though she had hated all-inclusive resorts, there was no cruelty or pain here, so she decided it was not hell. At least not in any meaningful way. Maybe a simulation. If so, she had led her life under the assumption that it was not a simulation, without proof one way or another, so she would continue to do so here. Her mind was less attached to such matters by now, and by the time she considered another possibility, that she was some sort of character in a movie or story (she couldn't be: no goal, no conflict, no arc), she realized it didn't really matter. She went with heaven, as it was simpler and freed her mind for other things.

Which other things were they? Rest? This was probably it, resting, peace, probably the benevolent reason for her diminished experience of herself in this heaven.

Once she made her choices, the questions left the foreground of her consciousness. She had a different relationship with knowledge in heaven. Knowledge was stored, and it stayed stored until you needed it, like the fat in your hips. Or like one of those storage units you rent when you downsize, where you never return, until one of your relatives is tasked with clearing out your belongings. She thought warmly of the relative who would have cleared hers, though she couldn't precisely see their face or what she had left in the storage unit. She could remember her eyes adjusting to the midday light, squinting once she stepped out of the unit. She remembered the stretch to pull down the garage door, how she'd had to push it down hard to get the last fifth shut, how difficult it had been for her to walk away from her things. But there wasn't much need for anything in heaven, so once she had that thought, it too was stored away from her consciousness.

As her thoughts were put away, one by one, she became lighter. Her phantom hunger weakened until it disappeared. She saw no need to return to the buffet, the part of heaven she liked the least. She walked farther away from the built-up part of the resort, the main building becoming smaller in the distance until there were only palm trees and the beach. And between two trees, there was a cream hammock, generous in material and embroidered like the hammocks where she had come from. She stopped and lay down and swung softly in the breeze.

With time (seconds? centuries?), she thought through her questions in her increasingly loose way. And the answers became sparser, and the words unrolled into pauses until they became breath, then continued unfurling themselves until they occupied no space or time and just were, by not being. The hammock stopped as she settled into a comfortable unknowing. And her thoughts stopped because there were no more questions. And as she was so still, time stopped too, for her. And she stayed there in her static time, and there she had it all at once. She faced the ocean as a child, after driving there for fifteen hours, on the first day of summer vacation, the ocean, the ocean. She was fourteen watching Almodóvar for the first time with her friends. And she was waking up in the sunny room, after their first night together; he was still sleeping, the city alive outside: a group of girls walked past laughing, the sound of the roll-up door of the coffee shop downstairs opening up. She was a toddler, her mom and dad holding each of her hands, helping her fly over the puddles. The splash. A warm plate of vatapá her mother and her aunts made for her. The hammock in the verandah at her aunt's summer house in Ilhéus. She was crossing the Manhattan Bridge alone, with the boats, the skyline, and that text on her phone. Curved concrete painted white. Picking up Ana at the airport. Laughing at her cat chasing the shadow of the fan. Something sprouted from her words on the page. The suitcase packed, the flower that grew in the crack of the sidewalk, the botanical garden conservatory tropical room in the winter, the short twisted trees of her hometown, cashews, caramel, rose water, the sun on her forearm, the smell of rain, his smell and hers. She was still. And time continued running, without her. Outside her stillness, she was no more.

## HELL

She always knew it would be Penn Station. Not the old Penn Station, with the 792 feet between the travertine floors and the metal arches and glass windows on the ceiling, filled with sunshine and air, gold rays pouring over fedoras in the old photographs. Not whatever the new Penn Station was promised to be either. No, this was Penn Station circa 2008. The ceiling middle-finger low; the only thing she could think of were stacked matchboxes. There were no new metaphors. Everything stale. No windows. Not a single one. She hated her job but needed to hang on to it. So many people had been laid off. Peter had been laid off and was having some sort of internal crisis. She thought he might be having an affair, and though she'd found out later she had been mistaken, she didn't remember that here, in hell. She was late for her train and had to rush, push through, run up the stairs. She wore high heels again, after so many years being done with them when she'd been alive. There were so many people, a faceless mass filling every space. She always missed the train. And the next train to NJ would take so long to come again. And the next train was always canceled. Accident on the tracks. And now it was midnight, and there was no place to sit. And though most people were gone, the cops hassled someone who had sat on the floor. And a cop nudged a man who had fallen asleep with the tip of his shiny black shoes. And she was reminded of why there were no seats: so people who had nowhere else to go would not be comfortable. So many people with nowhere to go, and it was winter. And it was summer and hot, and the platform where she waited for the 1, or the 2, or the 3 smelled like oil and urine. And the rats were not cute or funny or good company this time. And there was no music, nor children, nor dogs in bags this time. And she was never getting anywhere this time. This was Penn Station in 2015, and she was running again. And the tunnel from the E to the 1 was lined with so many American flags and cops leading everyone all the way to somewhere not good. There were no windows. And she ran for the train to NJ. She didn't like the suburb in NJ. She didn't like her job.

She felt guilty and she was guilty. There was no Devil, no talking, no regretting, only being, always forever. There was no fire for her. Things were not fair or proportional or reasonable. She missed the train. The cops kicked people awake. You could never sleep. This was Penn Station in 2016, election season. A drunk woman shouted at her, "Once he wins, you'll see." A man shouted at her, "Are you sure you need two slices of pizza?" Three drunk men in their twenties chanted "build the wall" for a few seconds and exploded in laughter. This time there were no protests, and she would never again feel her voice together with the voice of others, and their voices would never echo through and out of Penn Station. There was no justice, no peace. There was no hope. She knew what would happen, though her friends in the suburb didn't. She knew what would happen, even as she kept running up the stairs in her broken shoes, the left sole detaching. She was going to miss the train.

## PURGATORY

She had returned to LA from New York because her friend Ana was dying. When she'd lived in LA, she had not noticed how the California sadness permeated it whenever you sat still. Now all she did was sit still. She sat on a window seat, in the back of a city bus. None of her friends ever caught the bus there, but she did for years. And she did after seeing Ana. Ana had lost her hair and her eye and was on morphine. And yet they still laughed together, a couple of times, at the hospital. Some commonplace joke about the hospital food and the cafeteria in college, even though Ana wasn't really eating anymore, some old memory. Ana asked her to read for her. Anything, Ana said, whatever she had brought. Ana closed her eyes when she read, but if she stopped, Ana mustered a slight smile and asked her to keep going, please. She had come back from New York to see Ana before she died. Both knew Ana would die. And she did. Two days later, Ana would go into hospice at home. But that was later, and now she was stuck on the bus. It had been cancer for her too, like Ana, but it came for her so many years later. She had been lucky, she supposed. That was what riding a bus for eternity would do to you. You would think yourself lucky. Ana was not on the bus. Ana was in the hospital where she had just left her. And Ana had also long been dead, like her. And the bus kept riding, and it was always slightly overcast, but it never rained. The houses outside, all one-story buildings, were so low to the ground. Rows of teeth around a dolphin's mouth. A zoetrope, a carousel ride so long, you didn't notice the curvature, like driving down a straight road around the Earth. She had resented being stuck here, after spending most of her life on the East Coast. But at least she was not stuck in the New York subway during rush hour. This was what being still and moving for so long did to you: Sometimes you felt grateful. Other feelings came and went, like the houses. But gratitude settled better in that position, the stillness and the motion and the soft gray light. She leaned on the window and dozed off, counting the houses. When she woke up, nothing had changed. The bus never got to her stop.

{ }

The writer dreamed of her book. Of herself working on the book.
In the dream, she reread letters from her workshop, but they were
blank, then filled with childlike drawings: flowers, hearts, stars.
Gifts. One of the drawings was of a succulent, an intricate fractal
pattern. That one she knew was from the Devil. In the dream she
thought he remembered her problem: There were no concrete
nouns and many typos. She corrected them, but the y unfixed
themselves ont he ppage. She erased the paragraph. She wondered
if ghosts were real. And then she was a child at a large flat concrete
square, Praça dos Três Poderes, the congress right there. She was
facing the sculpture, a statue of two abstract human figures, *Os
Candangos*. They had no eyes.

She woke up with the sun beaming on her face and thought
of the lines "torso of steel / Winged elbows and eyeholes," which
Sylvia Plath had written about that same statue. Out the window,
the sun created a halo around the buildings and a flare, like an
old photograph. The city was empty but beautiful. Her desk was a
mess of marked drafts. She was grateful for the writing. The work
in progress. There was no progress outside. Everything was still.
She missed her workshop group. They were out there in the city

somewhere but felt so far away. She hoped they were doing OK. Jordan was taking long walks to cope. Marie took up handwriting letters, which she photographed and sent as JPEGs, as not to add to the risk faced by postal workers. They had not heard from Megan in a while, but Marie managed to confirm she was OK, as in alive and not sick.

The writer loaded the dishwasher. She reread her last paragraph and corrected a typo, adding the missing *d*, laughing momentarily at the dream, the words, the soul of things. She didn't know if the Devil would find his soul in stories, as he seemed to dream about. But there was something to his hunch. There was something there, in stories. There had been times in her life when she had been afraid of the page, and she knew there would be times when she would be afraid again. But now her fear was something else, bigger; it was outside in the world and in the room with Peter. On the page she could breathe; she could sprout, grow and tend; she could fix; she could cure.

The writer noticed something new on her pile of books close to the window. Succulents—mint green, brighter green, yellow, peach—arranged together into a tiny fractal garden.

{ }

The writer made a new ending for her story:

I was about to cry, and I didn't want her to see me this way. I went to the bathroom and cried quietly, hearing the muffled sounds from my dad's dubbed American movie, and, in the moments when the movie went quieter, my mother clearing the kitchen. I removed my glasses, and I wiped my eyes, washed my face and hands in cold water. Then, for a second, I thought I felt her, the ghost. It was as if she were there with me. In the mirror, a blurry version of my face, our face, mine, my mother's, the ghost's. We were all so sad. I cupped my cheek with one hand and touched the mirror with the other, our eyes, out of focus, met. I wanted to give the ghost a place, somewhere where she was welcome, for her sake, for my mother's sake, and for me. But I put my glasses back on, and she was gone. I ripped a piece of paper towel and wiped my fingerprints from the mirror. When I got back, I was going to revise the story. Give her a body of words. Bring her with me. Bring her home.

{　}

The writer was in a parking lot. The inside of her car was dark, except for the harsh light coming in at an angle from the light post on the left. Peter was inside the hospital, but she couldn't go in with him. Earlier that day, she had sat in a line of cars and gotten tested. There was a test now. When she'd first heard about it, she'd been afraid. They inserted something deep into your nose and scraped. It made her think of lobotomies. But the drive-through test she'd taken earlier wasn't nearly as bad as she'd imagined. One day people would be able to casually test themselves in their homes before heading to a party. It would take a year or more, the Devil had told her, or maybe the news had, but there would be a vaccine. The Devil had spoken of it with some hope but also with some grief. There was too much noise, and people didn't know how to listen. Something always got twisted or lost. The Devil had tried to tell them about the brain, hoping that understanding would help. He was sick of being blamed for things that could be fixed, with a little more understanding. The Devil told them about the brain, but they only ended up with the abomination of lobotomy. The writer had looked "lobotomy" up earlier that week (flashes of horrific figures in black-and-white from the movie *Häxan* came back to her as she had typed the word). An article labeled Dr. Walter Freeman, the great lobotomy enthusiast, as one of the most evil men in the world. The writer didn't know about that. He was evil beyond her comprehension. But there was tough competition.

Some of the other cars in the parking lot were empty, while others had people in them, waiting like her, but she couldn't see their faces. The writer dozed off in her seat.

She woke to an empty parking lot, except for her car. In front of her was Peter in his hospital bed, hooked up to the respirator, illuminated by the streetlights, as if he were on a stage. Stage right, entered the Devil, who focused intently on Peter. The Devil stood next to him, hovered his hand over Peter, and the bed and the respirator disappeared. The writer gasped. She was having trouble breathing. Peter needed the machine. He needed to breathe. The Devil kneeled on the floor and ran his hands over Peter's forehead, his cheeks. He sat on the ground and held Peter's limp body on his lap, reminding her of *La Pietá*. The Devil leaned in toward Peter's face, as if he were about to kiss him. Then their lips locked. The Devil did kiss him. No, the Devil was giving Peter breath. He breathed into Peter, and Peter's chest seemed to fill. And as he continued, the Devil's body started to lose its solidity; it was becoming transparent. The Devil was turning into a faintly red vapor. He was breathing himself into Peter, the vapor now a cloud, going in, in, diminishing itself as Peter was regaining his color, his chest getting back to its normal movement, up and down, until the cloud went all in.

She woke up with the first light of the morning, still in her driver's seat. There was a knock on her window. The parking lot was full. They needed the spot. She had to go home.

She couldn't find the Devil at home. She heard a noise in the kitchen, but it was only B. He had tipped over a glass of water. She wiped it and loaded it into the dishwasher. She replenished B's food and water. She showered and slept.

When she woke up, there was a voicemail. Peter was doing better, much better. She would probably be able to come get him soon. The Devil was gone.

# HASSELBLAD

## Triptych

### I.

There was Michele, and there was the girl. Michele held the door open. The girl carried an oversized backpack and wore frameless sunglasses with golden mirrored lenses. Michele could see a version of herself reflected in them, distorted, bathed in gold. A few strands of the girl's light-brown hair swayed with the breeze and shaped themselves as a moving frame around her face. The girl twisted off her backpack, leaning back and bending her knees slightly, which made visible the slender tone of her thighs. Her movements seemed part of a practice that had to be learned, like martial arts. Like dancing. Michele's body sensed a vague recollection of that motion. Though now her arms hung limply as the girl embraced her.

Michele and the girl were at the kitchen table. The girl held a caramel-filled cookie with the tips of her long thin fingers. She frowned a little, then smiled, brushing some crumbs from the corner of her mouth, incapable of making an ungainly gesture. Michele almost picked up a cookie but stopped herself and sipped her tea.

The girl talked about how Paris was for tourists and how she should have gone to Berlin instead. Then about a man, a lover, though she didn't call him that, with whom she had parted a few months ago. She had left him in Paris. Something in him had attracted her, she said. She didn't know what—maybe his crooked nose, or his broody mood, or the way he always looked irritated at her but could not resist her. But in the end, those things had ceased to be amusing, she said. She'd been bored of his monologues and diatribes on the emptiness of the art they went to see in the museums, his saying "derivative" with those cutting British *t*s. And how possessive he was. So she'd decided to leave him one morning, just like that.

"I hadn't closed the curtains after all the fighting the night before, and the sun woke me up," the girl said. "I looked at him while he slept." The girl looked out the window, and Michele followed her gaze as if they were both watching the boy resting his head on his pillow. "He was cute, but I was so sick of him. So much work." She sipped her tea, shaking her head slightly. "I had enough." She put her cookie down now and proceeded to talk about how she had disentangled herself from under his arm, afraid he would wake up, but his arm had just flopped and settled comfortably on the mattress. "I thought he might be dead. I poked him, then put my finger under his nose and detected his breathing. God, I was relieved!" The pitch of her voice was higher now. She took another bite of her cookie and laughed.

Michele laughed a little too, not knowing why, catching it from the girl like a yawn. She looked so young right then. Her appearance alternated between a child and an adult, depending on the angle and expression.

"I looked around the room, thought about my things in the closet, and felt, I don't know, lazy." She smiled. "He moved his arm again, and I freaked. I was so happy he didn't wake up. I thought, 'This is it, here's my chance.' I found my shorts but couldn't find my shirt. So I grabbed his, and my camera bag, my wallet, and my sunglasses, and I was out. I went down that spiral staircase so fast, I was dizzy." The girl giggled. "Downstairs, it was sunny and warm. I walked along the river for hours. I felt light. I felt, you know, free."

Michele could trace the shape of the girl's feelings inside her, an outline somewhere in her chest, a path carved by a stream of water that had since dried up.

"At some point that afternoon, I was walking by the river, and the sun was reflecting off ripples in the water, people were crossing the bridge as silhouettes, and a boat was about to go underneath it. I had this need, this hunger, for taking that picture, you know what I mean?"

Michele nodded. She did know what the girl meant.

"When I opened my bag, I realized I had his camera there. The Hasselblad he had been teaching me how to use. I grabbed it and told myself to just do it. And I knew what to do. It was incredible. I knew what to do the way I never had with him breathing down my neck. I knew to get the meter and point to the sky first. I knew to change the aperture and the shutter speed and not to worry about the ISO, which was fixed by the film. My fingers cupped around the lens and turned the aperture ring, and I let myself do it. I got out of my own way and took the picture."

The girl looked at Michele. Michele smiled and nodded, sincerely, and the girl's eyes were grateful.

"Later, I stopped by a street market. This guy" — she smiled wider — "was reading a book at his table. He sold records, used clothes, that sort of thing. Cute, kind of androgynous. I just loved him straight-away. I looked at him until he stopped reading, and I said hi," the girl said, reproducing her past flirtatious expression. "I bought a shirt from him and changed, took my shirt off right there, in the middle of the market." She had felt the sun and the breeze on her breasts and the orange heat behind her closed eyelids.

Michele sensed the shadow of that rush again. A fainter version of it, lingering like a phantom limb.

"I think some lady said, 'Mon Dieu!' The cute guy, Nico, laughed, which made me take my time with the shirt. Once I had it on, I looked at myself in the mirror." The girl had a satisfied look, as if seeing herself again now. Michele could see an old skinny mirror propped up against a clothing rack, a dusty blue fan at its feet, the strong sunlight reflected by its worn spotted face. "Then I threw my ex's shirt into Nico's little trash, with conviction." She brushed her bangs away from her eyes. "We ended up fooling around a couple of times. It was nice."

Michele, mimicking the girl, without thinking, grabbed a caramel cookie and this time took a bite too. The caramel was sweet and sticky; the crumbly cookie base became moist in her mouth. She let her eyelids grow heavy and fall shut, and for a second, it was just her, the caramel on her tongue, and her slow breath.

"But there was something not there, you know. It fizzled out." The girl sighed. "We just became good friends instead. When I left Paris, he gave me this."

The girl pointed to an old leather camera bag sitting next to her backpack on the floor, the kind Michele had once, a long time ago. The girl opened it to extract her camera. "Can I take a picture of you?"

She turned the dials and frowned a little, her face partially obscured by the camera. Michele had seen herself from that angle before when she'd tried to take a self-portrait in the mirror. But she hadn't been able to do it. She hadn't liked the look of her one eye closed tightly, wrinkled with exertion, unprotected by the camera. She had also been bothered by not being able to properly see the photograph as she took it, suddenly troubled by the prospect of that moment of complete darkness when the shutter closed. She'd tried to take the same picture with that exposed eye open, but the result looked unnatural, and it was difficult to see the same thing both from within the camera and free from it, at the same time. It had made her dizzy. Looking at the girl's face now, so young, so beautiful, she wished she hadn't worried so much and had just taken the picture back then.

"Nice." The girl clicked again. "Good."

## II.

Where had the time gone? One minute it was 6:00 A.M., and now it was suddenly noon. Michele had stayed up late and woken up early to clean the house. She had thought she'd finish before the girl arrived. But the twins had begged her to drive them to a game the day before, and this morning, the babysitter had called in sick. Michele had counted on her guest being late, but she was half an hour early, ringing the bell. Michele closed her eyes and breathed in slowly. She put on a smile and opened the door.

Her hand was still slightly slippery with soap, her fingers wet and wrinkled against the smooth round brass door handle. A damp tea towel hung over her right shoulder. The girl carried an oversized backpack and had on sunglasses with golden mirrored lenses, trendy, as Michele would've expected. They suited her though. Michele reminded herself not to get annoyed from the get-go. It was probably not the girl's fault she was early. Nor was it her fault they'd decided against sending the twins to that sleepaway summer camp. Nor that Ben had agreed to have the girl, his niece, stay while he was away on his work trip, as if Michele didn't already have enough people to look after, alone.

ANANDA LIMA

The girl twisted her backpack off, leaning back and squatting slightly. The way she did it seemed a little theatrical, as if she were performing for a seasoned traveler. Michele knew she was being catty. She took another breath and sustained her smile. The girl hugged her without conviction. Michele became aware of her hand still on the door handle. The other was now hanging by her side, holding the tea towel. She was not quick enough to hug the girl back before it was over, which made her feel rude and awkward.

"Come in. Come in." Michele whipped the tea towel back over her shoulder, extended her arm, and curtsied a little, like some caricature of a royal butler, and immediately regretted the ridiculous gesture. "Welcome!"

She stepped closer to the girl's backpack to bring it in for her. But it wouldn't move. It was as if it were stuck to the floor. She bent over and pulled hard. Felt a stab of pain in her lower back.

"Oh, don't worry, please. It's so heavy! I'll get it." The girl performed her action in reverse, squatting and leaning back first, threading her arms one at a time through the two loops, then standing up with that monstrous weight. She stood smiling with her backpack, the sunny day and the blue sky behind her, her hair moving slightly in the breeze.

The girl had grown a lot. Michele had seen her on family trips over the years but not recently. The girl had come to stay with them before, for a couple of weeks during a summer, interested in their proximity to New York City. She had been thirteen then. Michele couldn't believe it'd been ten years. The twins had been babies then, yes; it was around their first birthday. Michele had them relatively late, when she was forty-two, and they still felt like a fresh miracle then. The girl's face had been rounder, a kid's face. And she'd had a little acne on her cheeks and forehead (it embarrassed Michele to think in those terms,

156

but she couldn't help it), her hair always in a limp ponytail. Now the girl had turned out so pretty. And, unlike her younger version, she was also polite (she'd pretended not to see Michele's failed attempt to lift the bag). Michele wished she had hugged her back.

Michele took the girl to the kitchen and asked her to leave the bag there. "We'll take it up later." By "we" she meant Ben, something she didn't want to say because she knew it made her sound old-fashioned. But then she remembered he was not there.

Michele wondered what to give the girl. Lunch was nowhere near ready. The cookies from the twins' day camp bake sale sat on the sink. She got them out of their Glad Tupperware container (the kind in between reusable and disposable; Michele was never sure what to do with them). She arranged the cookies on a porcelain plate and asked the girl if she wanted some tea. The girl thanked Michele but declined. Michele offered coffee, and she accepted.

"So you've been all over . . . that's exciting!"

The girl smiled and nodded vigorously, her mouth filled with a cookie. "Uh-huh."

"Are you coming from Paris?"

The girl shook her head. "Uh-uh." She covered her mouth with her hand. "Berlin." She paused to swallow. "Paris was OK, but I don't know, it didn't seem like there's that much happening there. I mean, it was so touristy. This one morning, I was on my way to check out yet another overrated, overpriced sublet, and I just asked myself 'why?'" She took another bite and shrugged.

Michele was surprised to feel slightly hurt. She realized she'd looked forward to reminiscing about Paris with the girl. This small disappointment reminded her again of the girl's last visit. Susan, the girl's mother, who seemed to be in permanent competition with Michele, had told her the girl was interested in photography. Michele had given her an old camera and offered to teach her. She arranged a calendar full of photography exhibitions, contacted friends for a possible internship. The girl had taken the camera with an unenthusiastic "thanks" and declined everything else in favor of watching teenage romantic comedies in her room.

"So instead of going with that sublet," the girl continued, "I just texted a friend, and we took the train to Amsterdam. It was awesome. Then Berlin after that. Oh my God, Berlin was the best!"

The girl proceeded to talk about the "derivative, franchiseable emptiness" of the art scene in Paris. Michele remembered the teenage version of the girl lying on her stomach on the bed, her feet in the air. On TV, a former jock had watched a former nerdy girl—new hairstyle, no glasses—descend the stairs of her colonial, the former jock and her dad gasping at her beauty.

She imagined the girl looking at Michele and saying "derivative" in her high-pitched girlish voice.

"Weird, isn't it?" the girl said.

Michele had lost track and had no idea what the girl referred to. "Yeah," she replied.


Michele showed the girl upstairs to the guest room. She'd managed to make the bed, which was a queen this time, and clean the bedroom well enough. A mess sat behind the closed closet door, but the room looked perfectly organized on the surface.

The girl stepped in, walked to the window, and looked out. "Thank you." She sat on the bed and bounced a little, then stopped as if catching herself.

Michele noticed a pile of dirt, hair, paper, and dust bunnies she'd forgotten to collect, just outside the door. "Let me know if you need anything, OK?"

The girl nodded and thanked her again.

Michele closed the door and rushed downstairs to pick up the broom and dustpan.

The girl emerged downstairs seven hours later, when Michele and the boys were having dinner. The twins stopped bickering and stared in silence.

"Boys, go say hi to your cousin," Michele said, standing up to get the girl a plate. In the rush to get food ready before the twins turned into monsters, she'd forgotten to set a place for her.

"Hi," the twins said in unison, not getting up.

Michele motioned for them to rise, rolling her eyes for the girl's benefit. "I'm sorry, I wasn't sure you'd be joining us." Michele set the girl's plate on the table. "I thought you might be tired from your trip."

"Oh, don't worry," the girl said, hugging both boys at once. "I'm actually," she said, failing to suppress a yawn, "going out to dinner. I have a friend who lives near here, Madison? Or something like that." She stretched. "He's coming to pick me up." The girl asked for a towel, then went upstairs to get ready.

She came down again when Michele was loading the dishwasher. The girl was wearing mom jeans, a white T-shirt, and flat black leather shoes similar to something Ben would wear to the office, glasses with a round see-through plastic frame, and red lipstick. The outfit ought to look hideous, but somehow, the girl was stunning.

"You look nice," Michele said, with a clichéd rising intonation she had not planned.

"Thank you," the girl said, looking down at her phone. "Oh, my friend's here."

She said goodbye and headed out the door. Michele felt an uncontrollable urge to see who this friend was. Wasn't it also her duty? She walked toward the window but stopped short, thinking of how it would look. She went upstairs to find a room with the lights off.

"Mom?" Jack asked as she passed by their room, where he and his brother were watching a movie, a scary one by the sound of it. She thought of looking from there, but then the twins would ask her what she was doing. And they might follow her. She imagined the girl seeing the three little heads watching her. Just thinking about it made her blush.

She entered the darkened guest room in a hurry for the window, tripped over the girl's gargantuan backpack, and fell. She was able to break the fall with her hands, but the top of her head grazed the edge of the bed. "Shit," she thought she whispered, but it came out louder than she'd wished.

"Mom? Was that you?" Jack or Julian asked from their room.

Michele wondered if they heard her swearing. "Yes. Just me."

"Aunt Michele?" The girl's voice seemed to be coming from the stairs.

What was she doing back inside? Michele stood up quickly, and as soon as she did, the lights went on.

"Aunt Michele?" the girl asked, standing by the door with a surprised expression.

Without meaning to, Michele looked down at the girl's backpack, which lay twisted on the ground, one buckle opened. The girl's gaze followed hers and went back to Michele's face. Michele had looked at the bag because she had tripped on it. But now she thought the girl might think she was snooping, going through her things. Michele's face warmed. The girl was blushing too.

"I was just—" Michele swallowed. "I had forgotten . . . I was looking for . . ." She looked around the room. The closet. She opened it carefully and picked up the first thing she could pull out without causing an avalanche. An old photo album. "This."

"I forgot my wallet." The girl looked at her shoes. She mustered a faint smile and looked at Michele. "Also, I should ask you what I should do about getting back in later."

"Oh, yes." Michele held the album under her arm. "Come, I'll give you a set of keys."

The girl went out with her friend a few more times. He had never stopped by, but his name was Jean-Paul, and he turned out to be some sort of manager at one of his family's businesses, an electronics store. The girl showed up with presents she liked to show off (a sticker Instax, a mobile-phone photo printer) and leftovers from medium-range to expensive restaurants.

"So this Jean-Paul guy, he likes you, huh?" Michele asked one afternoon in the kitchen.

"Nah, we're just friends," the girl replied, opening the cupboard for a glass of water.

"So how do you know him?"

"I met him in Italy; his family is from there. He's a nice guy."

Michele didn't want to become the girl's mother. But it was difficult for her to tell what her responsibility, in this case, was supposed to be. She'd never had children that age. She asked Ben about it. He sent back a shrugging emoji. The next day, her sister-in-law sent her an email. It reminded her the girl was an adult. The girl's friend, Jean-Paul, was a friend of friends. The girl trusted her mother and told her everything. And her mother trusted her. Michele might understand one day, the girl's mother said. She hoped Michele would be able to cultivate such a relationship with her children too, a relationship built on mutual trust.

Michele wished she had not asked. The most embarrassing part was that she saw how ridiculous the situation was. The girl was a grown woman. But it was becoming harder for Michele not to think maternally of young people. When the girl had first come by as a teenager, the boys were so young, Michele didn't see her as belonging to the same category as them (children she had to protect and look after). The girl had been more of an annoying, bad-mannered guest then. Michele couldn't believe the twins would be thirteen themselves in two years. Sometimes these days, two years and five minutes felt like the same thing. The more the twins grew, the more the category of children expanded. Now, apparently, it encompassed college kids and young professionals. Paradoxically, the girl had not been a kid for Michele at thirteen, but she was one now at twenty-three.

Michele came downstairs and found her playing a card game with the twins. The girl put a card down, looking sheepish. The boys screamed and slammed their cards down. Julian scraped the pile in the middle for himself. They were all laughing.

The girl saw Michele looking at her, and her smile faded a little. She wrote the game's score down and stood. "Excuse me," she said, going around Michele and heading to her room.

She avoided Michele for the rest of that day and spent the next day in the city. But then she was able to behave in almost the same cordial way as before, though Michele still felt things were off between them. She thought of getting a sitter for the twins, taking the girl out for dinner and a show. But she didn't want to force things as she had the first time the girl stayed with them.

Michele came back from dropping the twins off at day camp one morning to find the girl on the couch, squinting in concentration as she examined an old camera sitting on her lap. The girl ran her fingers along its metallic edging, turned it around. It was a Hasselblad. Michele raised her hand to her mouth. It was such a beautiful camera.

"Wow," Michele said, walking toward the girl carefully with the gait of someone about to hold someone else's newborn. "It's gorgeous."

The girl smiled at Michele. "Isn't it?" She placed the camera on the coffee table, arranged it against a potted plant, and took a picture of it with her cell phone.

Michele was surprised that the girl's actions, that social media–post impulse, hadn't annoyed her. She could see it was a good composition. The grain of the table, the leaves, probably slightly out of focus, framing the Hasselblad, the window light hitting the arrangement at 45 degrees. The girl, the camera, the light. It was all beautiful. Michele wondered where she had stashed her own camera. She hadn't used it in months. And even then, it had been for the twins' birthday party. A different type of thing entirely.

"This is wonderful." Michele ran her fingers along the top to the rounded edge at the back of the camera. A 500C. "Where did you get it?" Michele asked out of genuine awe and curiosity but regretted it as soon as it came out, and she considered how it might have sounded to the girl.

"My friend Jean-Paul." The girl seemed a little more serious and paused as if figuring out whether to engage further or not. "It's a loan for a few days before they sell it at the store. They just got it as a trade-in."

"That's so great." Michele smiled at the girl, who looked at the camera. "Do you have film?"

"I don't know." The girl picked up the camera bag, looked inside briefly, and handed it to Michele.

Michele found a 120 millimeter roll. Her hand was positioned as a dancer's as she held it between her middle finger and thumb and turned it. She broke the seal. The backing paper was nice and clean. She picked up the camera, detached the film back, and removed the dark slide insert out. She turned the insert around so the back side faced the rear as it was supposed to (who'd been handling this camera before? Probably someone who'd used it for decoration. What a waste). She inserted the film in the take-up reel, fed it back, and locked it snugly into place. She lifted the magazine lever and started turning it. That sound of winding film—Michele closed her eyes and listened. She'd not touched a camera like this in so long, but before she could wonder about how to operate it, her body took over and remembered for her. She smiled and shook her head a little. She attached the back to the body again and lifted the camera, holding on to the weight and feel of its black surface and silver ridges against her fingers.

Michele remembered the moment she'd first taken a photograph with a Hasselblad on her own. She was in Paris, walking by the Seine. The sun was reflecting off ripples on the river, and people were crossing the bridge as silhouettes; a boat was about to go underneath. She wasn't experienced with the camera, but a hunger for taking that picture overtook her. She got her meter and pointed to the sky. Slowly, she played with the camera dials, changing the aperture and the shutter speed. She kept steady, looking through the viewfinder for several seconds. Then she took the picture, freezing it all into place. For the first time, she knew she'd gotten it right. She didn't have to wait to see it developed. She'd known.

"That was so cool." The girl looked at the camera and then at Michele, with a full smile.

"Yeah. Isn't it? I love these things."

"Me too! I'm in love."

Michele ripped up the tab of the film's cardboard box (400TX) and inserted it in the little window slot at the back of the camera.

"What was that for?" the girl asked.

"So we remember. So we know what kind of film we have in there."

"What kind of film?"

"ISO."

"Oh. Right."

"Do you wanna try it?"

"Yes!" The girl took the camera and looked at it with concentration.

"Oh, wait." Michele unclicked a metal holder and pulled the flat metal slider out of the camera.

"What was that?"

"It prevents you from taking a picture by accident. This"—Michele tapped on the film packaging—"is expensive."

"That's hard-core. It looks like those blades magicians slide through their boxes when cutting their assistants in half."

"Oh my God. Yes." Michele laughed. "OK, you know what to do?"

"I think so. But where are the dials?"

"I know." Michele laughed again, and the girl did too. "Look right at the base of the lens." Michele was going to set them, but she stopped herself and let the girl do it instead. "Shutter speed here. Aperture here."

The girl nodded and frowned in concentration again.

"They are interlocking," Michele continued. "So they change together. You know, if you open the aperture, the speed goes up; if you close the aperture, the speed slows down, keeping the same exposure."

The girl nodded, seeming to take some effort to process it but apparently following.

Michele turned one dial, and both women watched the other turn as a consequence. "See?"

"Oh!" The girl got it. "But then how do you . . . ?"

"Exactly. If you want them to operate independently, you have to click here. Then you can move one and not the other."

The girl pressed down and practiced moving the dials.

"And this is the . . ." Michele began to say.

"Focus," the girl completed. "How do you meter?"

"You need a light meter."

"Really? Cool."

"Did he give you one?" Michele looked at the bag. "No, it doesn't look like it."

"Oh." The girl looked disappointed.

"I have one, somewhere."

Michele went down to the basement.

When she came back up, meter in hand, the girl was holding her phone up. Moving it about, pointing it at different parts of the room. As Michele got closer, she realized the screen had an illustration of an old-fashioned meter on it, much older than the dusty one she held in her hand now. The simulated meter on the girl's screen was actually working, the dials changing depending on where she pointed.

"I found a light meter app," the girl said, excited.

"Can I see that?"

The girl handed her phone to Michele.

Michele loved the app. She wanted one too. "Here." Michele handed her meter to the girl. And they both pointed to the window, Michele with the girl's phone, the girl with Michele's meter. They compared their readings. They matched.

"OK. Now we are ready. You go."

The girl held the camera and looked around the room. She looked at the twins' skateboards in the corner, their shoes next to it. She looked at the mirror and at the glass chandelier. She settled on a pot of flowers on the coffee table and then stopped herself and looked at Michele. "Could I take a picture of you?"

The girl sat Michele by the window. A cloud had just covered the sun, and the light coming in was soft. She asked Michele to close her eyes and breathe. Michele thought of Paris and the bridge. She thought of the girl turning the dials now. She thought of the orange light behind her eyelids the time she'd changed her T-shirt in that street market. She thought of Ben and her lying in bed before the twins. And the twins as newborns. She thought of the idea of them as thirteen-year-old boys, a couple of years away. And she thought of the bridge again.

"Nice." The girl clicked. "Good."

### III.

The girl was sitting on the front stairs, looking at her phone, when Michele pulled up into the driveway. Michele was twenty minutes late. She'd just dropped the twins off at the airport to spend the summer with their father in Berlin. It took much longer than she'd thought. But she didn't want to miss time with her children for the sake of some small-time interview, some unknown kid's documentary. The girl smiled at Michele and gave her a little wave. She got up, put on a small backpack, and picked up a tripod. A roller camera bag stood behind her. The girl was dressed in overalls, the bottoms rolled up so that one could see her ankles going into her white sneakers. Predictably, a hipster (though she probably didn't call herself that, the label having become very uncool now). But still, the ensemble fit her. The golden mirrored sunglasses were especially charming. The twins would probably have gotten a kick out of seeing someone that cool coming to talk to their mom.

Michele wondered if she'd smeared her eyeliner. She'd surprised herself by crying on the drive back from the airport. It wasn't the first time the twins had spent the summer away from her. She'd been divorced for close to eight years now, and it was already Ben's fourth year in Europe. But there had been something about the way the twins looked standing in line. They were taller than the adults behind them. Their bodies were grown. And they didn't seem to need anyone anymore. Now she wanted to pull the sun visor down and make sure her eyes looked OK in the mirror. But she didn't want the girl to witness her doing that. She wiped the skin under her eyes as best as she could and got out of the car to greet the girl.

Michele brought a cup of coffee for herself and one for the girl into the living room. The girl instructed Michele to sit on her couch by the window. The girl sat across from her on the other side of the coffee table, between a video light (in a large octa softbox) and her camera (Canon 5D Mark IV with an external microphone), mounted on a tripod.

"Can you speak to the genesis of that project?"

The girl tried to maintain eye contact with Michele (so that she would in turn talk back and not look straight into the camera). But the girl failed to suppress a quick glance out the window. Michele guessed that was because of the lighting. Clouds were gathering outside, partially covering the sun. The girl was probably thinking about her exposure but didn't want to interrupt the ongoing rhythm of the interview. Michele looked out the window as she thought about that.

She thought about how it might seem to the camera as if she'd been thinking about the girl's question, which was probably nice in the footage. She looked back at the girl, who looked pleased.

Michele didn't have to think about the girl's question because she'd been asked similar questions many times. After a while, the interviews were all the same. Her beginnings, her initial deconstructions, *Confluences*, her embrace-of-the-derivative phase, *Sultured Screams*, and her final show in which participants were invited to burn the remainder of her work, anything she still owned. The supposed end of it, when she'd still been so young, her refusal to keep going. There were also the personal questions, brought under different guises depending on the publication: working with celebrities, the divorce, motherhood, giving up on her career in what seemed to be prior to a theoretical peak, etc., etc. It had been a while now, and things had completely phased out in the past couple of years. But Michele had repeated the routine so many times, it was still easy for her to follow the script.

"It grew out of an increasing dissatisfaction with my first works, which were silly and juvenile. Pretty photographs, representative, expected familiar narratives . . ." Michele could almost recite it all without listening to the words she was saying, like when the twins were little and she read bedtime stories to them while simultaneously composing the day's to-do list.

The girl nodded. Her eyes were sympathetic. Her pretty lips relaxed, slightly open.

From all the times before, Michele knew the interview might now turn to personal questions and would soon be coming to an end.

"OK. Now we will turn to some questions of a more personal nature, you know, just to illuminate some aspects of your work." The girl paused, as if testing Michele's reaction. She seemed to feel safe to continue. "After that, we'll wrap up. But do you need a little break, bathroom or anything, before we continue?"

"I'm fine, thank you. Do you need one?"

The girl giggled nervously. "Actually, I do. Do you mind if I use your restroom?"

Michele imagined the girl trying to memorize details of what she could see on her way to the bathroom. In Michele's mind, the girl opened her bathroom cabinets, hoping to see medicines, pills, or anything interesting. Michele didn't mind. She found the girl endearing, even if her approach seemed a little conventional for someone so young.

The girl came back, played with the camera, and set a bag next to her seat. She had a satisfied look. Maybe she'd found some dirt on Michele after all, which gave Michele a little thrill. But she couldn't imagine what the girl could have found. Either way, the girl certainly had something in mind. She'd perked up, sitting straight in her seat in anticipation. She was excited about something.

"OK, ready to start again?"

Michele smiled.

"I was doing a little research on your first project in Paris."

Michele nodded, a little disappointed. Nothing surprising. She would ask about the photographs she took of herself naked in public spaces. The girl kept talking. She mentioned the pictures. Michele started to wonder about what she should have for dinner that night.

"We all know about the work, the meaning of the project itself, and the role it played in your career," the girl went on. "What I am most curious about though is the small genesis and evolution of ideas in your work."

Maybe Michele could take advantage of her good relationship with the maître d' at Lorena's and convince them to let her get an order of the wild-caught Atlantic halibut as takeout so she could have it in her pajamas while watching Netflix.

"For example, I am wondering about this story I heard about a time before you started working on that project," the girl said.

Michele was confused. What was the girl talking about now?

"I heard you took off your shirt right there, in the middle of the market." The girl laughed. She was trying to bring Michele in, as if they were old friends reminiscing about the story. "You threw it in the trash and put on your new shirt."

It took a minute for Michele to understand what the girl was saying. She knew the story, of course, but she couldn't make sense of the girl telling it to her. There was a long pause. She realized her face was scrunched up in confusion, but she couldn't help it. How would the girl know? How would anyone know?

"I tracked down someone in Paris."

Michele gasped. Nico. How?

"Juliette Bois, daughter of Nicolas Bois."

Michele raised her hands to her mouth. They were trembling.

The girl picked up the bag next to her and pulled something out of it. A box. She opened it and pulled out a photograph. "She gave me this." She slid it across the coffee table.

Michele ran her fingers over the photograph of Nico, his delicate little nose, his eyes squinted, a cigarette dangling from his mouth. He had an arm around Michele, young and beautiful, laughing in profile.

Michele looked at the girl, happy between her camera and her video light. And she didn't feel angry or trapped (even though that was what it had been, a trap). She was grateful for what the girl had given her. "Thank you."

"She also gave me this." The girl held another photograph, this time more carefully.

Michele waited for her to slide it across the table, but the girl hesitated. It was as if the girl had forgotten what her plan was. Or as if she had it all planned but was now afraid of going through with it. The girl glanced at the camera and at the window. The light was decreasing, the afternoon coming to an end. It was as if the girl was now on the same clock as Michele and had finally realized how quickly time went by. She handed it to Michele.

It was that first picture she'd taken with the Hasselblad of that bridge in Paris. An underexposed boat about to go underneath it, the sky almost burned white. On top, tiny silhouettes of the passersby. The whole thing was a little out of focus. Not the worst photograph one can take, but still not a good one. Michele laughed.

"You thought all your photographs had been burned," the girl said.

"No. Just the ones I still owned."

"This one is yours now."

Michele wondered if the girl understood what the burning of the photographs had meant. When Michele began to be recognized, and her work became collectible, when it was featured in museums, it underwent a transition. Before then, when she'd been just a regular person with a camera, every copy of a photograph was just as worthy as another. She could make as many copies as she wanted from the negative. If a print got damaged, it didn't matter. But to be collectible, Michele was made to impose restrictions and tie the images back to their physical manifestations. She had to print limited editions to impose on them a rarity that would justify their price in a gallery. The collectors and curators could then pretend her photographs were more like paintings than like the reprintable words of fiction. But Michele had wanted to set them free of their physical forms again. By burning the so-called originals, she elevated the status of all the reproductions and digitized copies. The photographs became more like concepts than pieces of paper. Loss or damage to any individual physical print could no longer threaten them. It was as if she'd turned them from bodies into souls. She was pleased she didn't feel she had to explain that to the girl now. She was OK with her not understanding it. Michele had come a long way over the years; she could see that now.

"You know what we'll have to do, right?" Michele asked.

The girl nodded with a mischievous smile.

"Hang on. I don't want to set the house on fire." Michele got up and looked around the kitchen closets. She came back with a large pan with a lid and a lighter.

"Do you want to do it?" Michele asked.

"I was wondering if you could," the girl replied.

Michele had not burned any of the old photographs herself. She'd asked museum patrons to do it as part of that final exhibition. She understood now, that decision had not just been about making the show interactive. She could not have done it herself then. She'd still been attached to them. But she no longer felt that way. Plus, this one photograph brought by the girl was different. It had not been collected or exhibited or digitized, as far as she knew, which made its burning an event of a different nature and, in a way, more significant. A version of the photograph would stay in Michele's memory, and Michele trusted that the version in the girl's memory, and in Nico's children's memories, would eventually become different from hers. By burning it, she would ensure that this one photograph, her memory of the picture, would be hers alone; it would perish when her body did. Michele looked down at the picture and the lighter and the girl and her suburban house. She looked at the Hasselblad up on a shelf, reduced to decoration (how she had mocked people who did that and how delicious it was to be one of them now). She was happy. She liked the idea of trading places with the girl in this way. She could do this now, and it would cost her nothing.

"OK. I'll do it. As long as I do it like this." Michele faced the back of the photograph to the camera.

"I like that," the girl answered, seemingly excited by Michele's eccentricity.

"And . . ."

"And?"

"You won't keep any reproductions or include any footage of the content of the photograph in the film."

The girl considered this, then nodded. "I have a scan." She looked into Michele's eyes. "I'll delete it."

Michele knew she just had to trust the girl. She knew now that she could only do her part of the work as she wanted and what happened after that was beyond her control. She also knew someone else, Nico's daughter or any number of people, could have a copy. They could just as easily not have it, given how unremarkable the photograph was. Michele could only work with the information and guesses she had. That was the only way anyone could do anything.

"One more thing." The girl paused and unzipped her backpack, taking out another Canon, a film one this time. "Can I take stills of you as you do it?"

Michele nodded. She held the flame next to the photograph, careful not to look at the camera.

"You can look at me," the girl said. She waited for Michele to comply and clicked the shutter. "Nice." The girl mimed so that her praise would not interfere with the video footage. "Good."

{    }

You probably could not tell by looking at her now, squinting at the morning sun as she walked out through the hospital sliding doors, but once, in her twenties, the writer had slept with the Devil. It was Halloween, and she wore all red. She was "Inauguration Nancy Reagan." Thinking about it now, the writer was proud of her costume, as was the woman she had been that night in her amber-lit prewar NYC apartment, smoothing the sides of her red dress around her hips in the mirror propped against the brick wall. The writer zipped her puffy navy winter coat and paused in front of her reflection on the glass exterior of the hospital. Her eyes were tired; the strays on her messy high bun were made golden by the bright sunlight. The writer and the young woman smiled at their reflections, together across time.

Sometimes the writer could still see the young woman's face hiding in hers. She could see it now in her blurry reflection on the window, their faces faintly superimposed. The young woman's face had been sharper. The writer's outline was softening. Almost as if the young woman's face had been the present, and the writer's, the fading past. Almost as if the writer's face were the draft, and the young woman's face, the finished work. But it was in this shape, with boundaries less defined, that she found herself and her writing. The closer you looked at something, the harder it was to see simple clear lines. Like looking at a painting, really close. Like objects that appear to touch but, when considered at an atomic level, never really touch (almost touching, and always touching, all at the same time).

Later, she would see the Devil in crowds or among the extras in movies, but it was always so fleeting, she was never sure. She would think she heard him in her mind, but it was only her own thoughts, so used to talking to him. And sometimes she would search for him in Peter's eyes, when they lay in bed together, but she didn't know how to tell.

The Devil had never asked for the writer's soul. He didn't want anyone's soul. All he wanted was his own. Maybe, the writer wrote, one day he would have what he wanted. He would grow and tend it; he would get it to sprout from his stories, the telling, the words, the spaces in between.

# Acknowledgments

Thank you to my editor, Ali Fisher, for engaging with this book with such generosity and brilliance, for joining and supporting me in my love for literary shenanigans, and for making the process so joyful. Thank you so much to my wonderful agent, Sarah Bowlin, for your guidance, company, and beautiful sensibility. Thank you to everyone at Latinx in Publishing and Macmillan for the great gift that was the WIP fellowship, with special thanks to Nan Mercado and Manuel Gonzalez, for your kindness, and for believing in me and my work.

Thank you to the whole team at Tor for your wonderful work in bringing this book into the world, including Dianna Vega, Giselle Gonzalez, Rachel Taylor, Jessica Katz, Manu Velasco, Rafal Gibek, Steven Bucsok, Will Hinton, and Devi Pillai. Thank you to the amazingly talented Jamie Stafford-Hill for the incredible cover that is so perfect for the book.

Thank you so much Vanessa Chan, Julia Fine, John Keene, Gwen E. Kirby, Eric LaRocca, Kelly Link, and Kevin Wilson for your beautiful words about the book. Thank you, Beowulf Sheehan for the beautiful photograph.

Thank you to everyone at the Sewanee Writers' Conference for your work, friendship, and support. Thank you, Gwen E. Kirby, for so many laughs, for your writing, for trying in vain to teach me how to make a drink (#swcbarforever), and much more. Thank you, Leah Stewart, for using your brilliance to do so much good (on the page and in real life). Thank you, fellow photographer and friend Alyssa

Konermann (I am so lucky to be in a duo with you), Sakinah Hofler, Shelby Knauss, Nathaniel Nelson, Jonathan Bohr Heinen, Adam Latham, Kate Jayroe, Briana Wheeler, Phillip Christian Smith, Chelsea Whitton, Pritha Bhattacharyya, Bea Troxel, Norris Eppes, Anessa Ibrahim, and Cianon Jones.

Thank you to my friends and teachers at the Rutgers University-Newark MFA Program where many of these stories began. Thank you, John Keene, for your generosity, genius, and words. Thank you, Alice Elliott Dark, Cathy Park Hong, James Goodman, Jayne Anne Phillips, Rachel Hadas, Akhil Sharma, Sarah Nicholls, Rigoberto González, Melissa Hartland, the original fantastics (Aiden Angle, Andrew Erkkila, Andy Gallagher, Josh Irwin, Lauren Parrott), Simeon Marsalis, Brian Loo, Madani Sheikh, Ryan Wong, Ariel Yelen, Diana Li, Emily Caris, Emily Luan, Grey Vild, Nhu Xuân Nguyễn, Ricardo Hernandez, Susanna Velarde Covarrubias, Tracy Fuad, and the classes of '18 and '20.

Thank you to Disquiet International for awarding me with a FLAD fellowship, for your support and great times, and to all my fellow Luso workshop friends, with a huge obrigada to our fearless leader, Katherine Vaz. Thank you also to the Tin House, Community of Writers, and Bread Loaf summer conferences for all I learned there and the wonderful summers. Thank you to everyone who participated in our Maplewood writers' group (aka WAAK, WWADS, or mom's night), including Kathryne Squilla, Alyson Levy, Giovanna Fernandes, Hadas Almagor, Jennifer Rondeau, Miriam Reimer, and Shari Astalos. Thank you to the wonderful people and writers who welcomed me so warmly into the Chicago community. Thank you to so many more friends who supported me and inspired me during the writing of this book (though I can't name you all, I am so grateful you are in my life).

Thank you to the publications and presses where earlier versions of the stories in this book first appeared: *Witness* ("Rapture"), *Kenyon Review Online* ("Antropófaga"), *Passages North* ("Ghost Story"), *Apogee* ("Tropicália"), *Pleiades* ("Hasselblad: Triptych"), *Kweli* ("Idle Hands"), *New South* ("Rent"), and *Green Mountains Review* ("Porcelain") and the chapbook *Newfound* ("Tropicália"). Thank you to the wonderful editorial team in these publications, including fabulous and generous editors Crystal Odelle at *Newfound* and Miriam Alexander-Kumaradoss at *Apogee*.

Thank you to my loves Noah and Dan Shiber who are everything. And thank you, reader, for joining me in these stories.

# About the Author

**ANANDA LIMA** is a poet, translator, and fiction writer born in Brasília, Brazil, now living in Chicago, Illinois. She is the author of the poetry collection *Mother/land,* winner of the 2020 Hudson Prize. Her work has appeared in *The American Poetry Review.*